Cooking is Murder

A Myrtle Clover Cozy Mystery, Volume 11

Elizabeth Spann Craig

Published by Elizabeth Spann Craig, 2019.

This is a work of fiction. Similarities to real people, places, or events are entirely coincidental.

COOKING IS MURDER

First edition. August 7, 2019.

ISBN: 978-0997168563

Written by Elizabeth Spann Craig.

For my sister, Mary Ligon Spann Peterson.

Chapter One

"Cooking school?" asked Miles. He appeared to be trying very hard to think before he spoke.

"No, no, Miles. Not just cooking school. This is more of a class for experts to become even *better* and to learn new techniques. More of a grad school for cooks, in a way," said Myrtle. Her white hair stood on end like Einstein's, which seemed to emphasize her enthusiasm.

Miles's face held a very cautious expression. He pushed his rimless glasses up his nose. "This class was something that you signed up for all by yourself?"

"Well, *certainly*. Don't you understand how classes work? It's not as if I received a letter in the mail telling me that I'd been signed up for the course without my knowledge. It's not *jury duty*."

"Red didn't have anything to do with this, then?" asked Miles.

"Not a bit. You know that I automatically try to get out of everything that Red signs me up for because he seems adept at digging up busywork for me. This is something to do for fun. Elaine mentioned it to me. It was to be one of her many hobbies, but she had a conflict for this one. She'll be in the car driving Jack to preschool when it starts. But I thought that *you* might want to do the class with me. It would be more fun with a friend there and you like to cook."

Miles knitted his brows. "I wouldn't say I liked to cook as a *hobby*, though. I wouldn't have said that *you* liked to cook as a hobby."

"That's one of the best things about retirement, Miles. We get to develop our skills. Who knows? I could be the next celebrity cook. For heaven's sake. Have you got indigestion or something today? You've had the oddest expressions cross your face in the last five minutes. I've got Pepto-Bismol if you need it."

He shook his head. "Where did you say this class was?"

"I didn't. It's at the community college."

"Which is not exactly within walking distance," noted Miles. "I now see behind your flattering desire to have me enroll in the class with you. I have wheels."

"Whatever. I think you'll enjoy it. Pure and simple. The instructor is Louvenia Defore."

Miles said, "I think I know who she is, but I didn't realize she was a master chef."

"I don't recall saying that the class was taught by a master chef. This is Bradley, North Carolina, not Atlanta, Georgia. The class will be taught by a frequent blue-ribbon winner at the county fair."

"Got it," said Miles a bit wearily. He paused. "What day is it taught? I might be busy that day. Or have a conflict." His voice indicated hope that some sort of obstacle might happily appear.

"It's *all* the days. It's a two-week, everyday class. That way we build up our expertise quickly. And I know you're not busy because you were just commenting yesterday that you had such a quiet stretch coming up," said Myrtle, beginning to get cross.

There was a resounding explosion in Myrtle's yard, followed by yelling. Myrtle sat impassive in her armchair, hands folded neatly in her lap, as if nothing out of the unusual had happened at all.

"Should we check on Dusty?" asked Miles, glancing toward Myrtle's front window. "I'm assuming that it was Dusty's yard equipment making that noise. Did something blow up?"

Myrtle sighed. "No need. It's just that ancient lawnmower of his. My very generous son offered to help get him a new one but Dusty seems to enjoy the drama every week provided by the backfiring mower."

"That was nice of Red," said Miles.

"It was more that Red didn't want to have to take over the general maintenance of my lawn. He seems to think that being police chief in Bradley takes up too much of his time. Red always said that he didn't want to pay for parts for Dusty's mower, but then the mower got worse and worse. As the mower got worse, it got noisier. It used to be a much quieter mower than the modern mowers, but with Dusty 'repairing' it, the noises it was making were so loud it was waking my grandson up from naps." Myrtle rolled her eyes. "Although Red should be able to mow my grass every now and then. It's not as if he's even *doing* anything most of the time. So! Back to the class. As an extra added inducement, I've decided that we'll reward ourselves by showing off our cooking skills at a dinner party. A soirée." She peered more closely at Miles. "You've got the oddest expression on your face. Are you *sure* you're feeling well? Anyway, I think it will be a lot of fun."

Miles said weakly, "Won't it all be rather expensive? And I thought soirées involved music and dancing."

"Our soirée will be music-free. And I'm going to save some money by serving coffee instead of a bunch of wine. That way we can all talk about the wonderful food and the myriad of tastes we'll provide. And—pooh. You've got plenty of money. You're practically rolling in it."

"I assure you that there is no rolling going on," said Miles primly. "And at our age, perhaps it would be wise to save up for rainy days. Considering our fixed incomes and all."

"You're rolling in it compared to me. A retired accountant versus a retired teacher? Please."

"Retired *engineer*," said Miles stiffly.

"Anyway, the point is that I promise the class isn't expensive and we'll pick foods for our dinner party that won't be expensive, either. And there's no point saving up for a rainy day. There's been *no* rain here for quite some time. We're in a drought, remember?" asked Myrtle.

"That wasn't exactly what I meant."

"Of course it wasn't, Miles. But I'm getting impatient. Come on ... it'll be fun."

He appeared to be thinking things through for a few minutes. He pushed his glasses up his nose and slowly said, "You know, cooking school isn't a bad idea. Not at all. After all, there's definitely room for improvement. But I want nothing to do with the dinner party or whatever it is. I'm only saying yes to the class."

Myrtle nodded, smiling now that she seemed to be getting her way, at least in terms of the cooking class. "Fine, fine. If you don't want to be a partner in an historic dinner party, that's up to you. But the class will be fun. And we'll know everyone in there."

Miles raised his eyebrows. "Will we? How do you know?"

"Because we know everyone in town," said Myrtle with a small shrug. "Easy. That's one of the benefits of living in a place like Bradley."

Miles looked as though he wasn't completely convinced this was an actual benefit of his town.

The door flew open, smacking the wall behind it, and Dusty, looking more disheveled than usual in fraying, grass-stained khakis and a torn undershirt, stomped in. His thin, gray hair was pasted to his high forehead with sweat, dirt, and oil. "Blasted lawnmower," he muttered, heading for Myrtle's kitchen. He nodded in greeting to Miles, who lifted a hand to wave at him.

"Halt!" roared Myrtle, standing up from the sofa imperiously. "Dusty, you're tracking in half of the Great Outdoors into my house."

"Puddin'll take care of it," grumbled Dusty, looking toward the kitchen with the fixation of a pointing hound dog.

"Puddin? Cleaning? You know it's impossible to get your wife over here to clean. Even if I manage to wrangle her in the house, she only wants to watch soap operas and pillage my fridge. What exactly is it that you need and I'll get it for you?"

"Glass of water," said Dusty, glowering at Myrtle. "Or somethin' stronger, if you've got it."

"I'll just ignore that last bit since you'll be driving your equally-decrepit truck out of here after mowing my lawn. My son *is* the police chief, after all. I need to make sure that law and order is maintained—at the very least in my own living room," said Myrtle, walking over to the kitchen.

Dusty's expression grew wily at the mention of Red. "Your Red done told me he'd git me a new mower." He perched on the arm of Myrtle's sofa.

"Which you've always refused. It's like the care and feeding of that dilapidated lawnmower is your horrid little hobby or something." Myrtle handed him the water and waved him off the sofa arm. "Dusty, you're just too ... dusty ... to sit on my upholstery right now. How about the stool?"

Dusty loped over to a stool in the corner, leaving a trail of debris in his wake like a comet. "I'm done finished with that thing now. Reckon he'll still gimme another mower?"

"You don't mean to tell me that it's finally kicked the bucket? In the middle of mowing my yard?" Myrtle's face was horrified.

"It's kaput," said Dusty succinctly, taking a gulp from the glass. "But it weren't in the middle of mowing."

"Oh, good," said Myrtle, sinking down in relief.

"It were at the beginning," said Dusty.

Myrtle stood back up and walked over to the window. The tall grass was indeed still there. Even more terrible, Dusty had apparently been able to mow Myrtle's ghastly neighbor's lawn before coming to Myrtle's house. Erma's yard, despite being covered with crabgrass and chickweed and other scourges, looked better than hers now. That was patently intolerable.

"I'll call Red now," said Myrtle hurriedly. "I can't have this nonsense when I'm hosting a dinner party here."

Miles gave Dusty a glum look as Myrtle strode to the kitchen for her cell phone.

Dusty asked in a low voice, "Who's cookin' the food? Not her, right?"

Miles said, "I strongly suspect it will be Myrtle, yes. I'm going to try to distance myself from the actual food as much as possible."

Dusty grunted. "Good luck. Hard to do, if yer a guest." He stared at a brightly-colored object near Myrtle's desk. "Whut is *that*?"

Miles glanced over and very quickly glanced away again. "Don't remind me of that. It's something Red's wife made. Elaine has these hobbies. They never go well"

Dusty stared at it in fascination. "Looks like somethin' to chase evil spirits away."

"It's a *gnome*," said Myrtle sharply as she walked back into the room.

"Don't look like yer other yard gnomes," said Dusty. "Whut happened to it?"

"Elaine happened to it. She's been dragging Red and Jack around to flea markets and garage sales and finding things that need to be refurbished or restored. Then she does ... that ... to them. Paints them and whatnot," said Myrtle.

Myrtle and Dusty stared at the gnome while Miles averted his eyes. It was very brightly colored and seemed to have an evil, leering expression on its face. Its hands were held out in front of it as if it were begging.

"It's hideous," said Miles.

"I'm fairly certain that it wasn't even attractive in its original condition," said Myrtle, tilting her head to study the gnome. "I'm not sure that it was even a gnome. It looks more like a troll to me."

"Do you even care what it looks like?" asked Miles. "After all, the whole point in dragging your collection of yard gnomes out in the yard is to get Red's goat after he's made you mad about something. Having that ghastly thing out in your yard should certainly qualify as something to make him mad."

Myrtle said, "I couldn't even bear to subject my other gnomes to this one's presence. And now the problem is that Pasha loves sitting on it so much. I've got to figure out what to do with it."

Pasha was the feral black cat who'd befriended Myrtle.

Red gave a brief knock and walked in. He was wearing his police uniform and his red hair looked a bit more streaked with gray than usual. He nodded a greeting to Miles before saying to Myrtle and Dusty, "Now Mama was a little confusing on the phone. Something about a dinner party and a problem? I can just imagine the problems that could escalate with my mother and a dinner party."

Miles gave a hiccupping laugh that was halfway between a giggle and a cough.

"So I can only imagine," continued Red, "that the call had something to do with the fact that the yard is only half-mowed and that dinosaur of a mower is sitting in the middle of the jungle."

"It done broke," said Dusty. "Can't do no more mowin.'"

"All right. I promised you a mower and I'll get you a mower," said Red. "But I can't do it right this second. I've got to go see Mr. Terry and it can't wait."

"What on earth is wrong with Mr. Terry that could possibly constitute more of an emergency than the fact my yard is a complete eyesore?" demanded Myrtle.

"He's trapped in his house by a feral pig," said Red. "That pig is totally obsessed with him. This whole past week it's been circling his house off and on, snorting and baring his teeth. Mr. Terry needs to go to the grocery store and thinks the pig is going to attack him as soon as he leaves the house."

"Sounds likely," said Miles thoughtfully. "Those feral pigs can be vicious."

"I'll be trapping and relocating it. Then I'll maybe have some time to research mowers and see what's in my price range. I'm not made of money, unfortunately," Red said to Dusty. Dusty nodded, a skeptical look on his face. Compared to Dusty, Red was *decidedly* made of money.

Myrtle pursed her lips unhappily. "Don't we have animal control for animals that need to be controlled?"

"Mr. Simmons is taken by a fever," said Red. "And I don't especially want to be exposed to it or pass it along to everybody else."

Myrtle sighed. She certainly didn't want little Jack, her grandson, to catch a fever. But she hoped that Red could find her a mower by the end of the day.

Red was heading back out the front door but paused and turned around. "And I'm very interested in hearing more about this dinner party, Mama."

"You'll hear all about it, I'm sure. I might even expand my cooking. Greener Pastures is always looking for entertainment, you know. I could do a cooking demonstration there," said Myrtle.

Red said quickly, "That will violate Health Department regulations."

"You're making that up," said Myrtle, eyes narrowed.

Miles tried to change the subject. "Greener Pastures did have wonderful food."

Red said, "That's what I'm saying. I keep trying to convince Mama of all the great reasons she should be a resident there."

Myrtle said sharply to Miles, "I well remember your love of their food. If you think it's so great, you should move in there yourself."

Miles shook his head. "After a bit more digging, I discovered it wasn't a good fit for me."

"Too many flirtatious widows?" asked Myrtle.

Miles gave her a cold look. "The library there didn't have any books for me. It was all *Jennifer's Promise* and that sort of thing. It was like they didn't accommodate their male clientele at all."

Myrtle said, "That's because they pass away so quickly. Men don't live as long as women, you know. Why make the investment?"

Red said quickly, "Okay, on that note I'll take my leave."

"I'll tell you more about the dinner party soon. And you'll be invited of course," said Myrtle grandly.

Red and Miles shared an inexplicable look before Red quickly left.

Myrtle hadn't given Miles much time to think about the class. The registration deadline was the following day and the class started directly after that.

Miles was rather grim while driving to the community college. "It's very strange going to school again. I have the horrible feeling that I'm going to spend tonight besieged by nightmares about forgetting my high school locker combination."

"At least you *had* lockers," said Myrtle with a sniff. "That must have been some fancy high school. This is a college though, so there shouldn't be any memory jogging jolts."

The community college was an older one with ivy crawling up many well-worn brick buildings beside several brand-new looking ones. There were quite a few students there and the parking lot was full enough for Miles to have to make more than one pass through it.

"It must appear as if you and I have taken an exceedingly long time to get a diploma," murmured Miles as they walked among a throng of twenty year olds.

"Don't be silly! We're role models. We're demonstrating that education is lifelong. Think of it, Miles. When we leave this school, we'll have mastered a few dazzling cooking techniques."

Miles said carefully, "You're very optimistic about our results. Just remember that you and I don't do a lot of sophisticated cooking. Maybe we'll end up being hopeless as students."

"Speak for yourself," said Myrtle, raising her eyebrows. "I'm approaching this experience with an open mind. Now where's the Harris Building? That's where we're supposed to be going." She stopped in the middle of the sidewalk, craning her neck to look around as she leaned on her cane.

A young woman, weighed down with what looked like an impossibly heavy backpack, stopped beside them. "You're looking for the Harris Building, ma'am? It's right back there. You passed it, actually. It's near where you parked."

Myrtle beamed at her. "Thank you, sweetie." As the young woman walked away and Myrtle and Miles turned around, Myrtle said, "What a nice girl. That was kind of her to help a stranger."

"We probably remind her of her great-grandparents," said Miles glumly. "We really stand out. We're not wearing backpacks. That's the thing, apparently—backpacks. And headphones. We have neither. Nor tattoos or piercings. Those are popular items, too."

Myrtle chose to ignore him. "Oh, there's the Harris Building. And ...."

Her voice trailed off and she came to a complete stop when she spotted the gaunt figure standing on the sidewalk ahead of them.

Chapter Two

Myrtle gasped. "Wanda! What on earth are you doing way out here?"

Miles unconsciously patted his wallet. Wanda, a psychic who lived in perpetually dire straits, was a cousin of his. A rather needy cousin. He said absently, "Surely we're closer to Wanda's house than we are to our own. Wanda *lives* far out."

Wanda, wearing dark pants that hung on her thin frame and an equally ill-fitting top, grimaced in greeting. "Decided I'd come by."

"But *how*?" spluttered Miles. "I didn't even know I'd be here *myself* until Myrtle railroaded me."

"Because she's psychic, Miles. For heaven's sake, don't you pay attention?" said Myrtle with asperity. She looked at Wanda with a critical eye. Wanda had gone through a spell where she didn't only look thin, but looked as if she wasn't feeling well to boot. Myrtle was relieved to see that her friend was looking strong and much less frail than she had been. "Wanda, you're looking well."

Wanda nodded. "Writin' horoscopes pays good," she said gruffly. "And done stopped smokin'."

Miles, always somewhat afraid he might end up on the hook for Wanda's healthcare, looked relieved. "Well now, that *is* good news. You've got to be feeling so much healthier and better."

"More fidgety and nervous," Wanda said with a shrug of a thin shoulder. "But eatin' better with that good money from the paper."

Myrtle supposed that Wanda's new gig at the local paper paid more than she and her brother had been making selling fortunes, peanuts, and live bait from their remote home off a rarely traveled highway. Although she suspected that most people wouldn't call the money 'good.'

Miles said somewhat uneasily, "But what are you doing here, Wanda? You weren't planning on attending class with us, were you?"

Wanda looked at him solemnly with unblinking dark eyes. "Had a message fer you."

"For Miles?" asked Myrtle with great surprise. "But usually the messages are for *me*. You're always trying to relay that *I'm* in danger."

Wanda said, "I got a general-purpose message, too. '*A crust eaten in peace is better than a banquet partaken in anxiety.*'"

Now Myrtle and Miles both gaped at Wanda.

"What's that ... Shakespeare?" asked Miles of Myrtle, the retired English teacher.

"I rather think it's Aesop," said Myrtle thoughtfully. Then she demanded, "Wanda! What on earth do you mean?"

Miles suddenly smiled. "She's obviously against your dinner party plans, Myrtle."

"What's the message relating to Miles? And why are you suddenly so concerned about him? And how did you find this quotation?" asked Myrtle, hand on her hip as she leaned on her cane with the other.

Wanda shrugged again. "It's th' sight." She said to Miles, "Yer in danger."

Miles gulped.

"You never look that concerned when *I'm* the one in danger," said Myrtle to Miles with irritation. She sighed. "Now he's going to go into cooking class with a suspicious attitude."

"I'd imagine there'd be a lot of knives in cooking class," said Miles unhappily.

Myrtle said, "The irritating thing about your fortune telling, Wanda, is that you don't really have any specifics for us. Is Miles in danger at the cooking class? At my dinner party? Or at home, blissfully unaware as he digs into a salad tainted with listeria?"

Miles groaned, putting a protective arm around his stomach.

Wanda growled, "I'm just sayin' for him to keep his eyes open."

"And you've got *nothing else*? The sight didn't just toss some other random tidbit at you that you weren't totally sure how to interpret?" asked Myrtle.

Miles peered anxiously at Wanda.

Wanda gave this a little thought, mulling it over in her head. Then she said, "People is clumsy."

"Well, I guess that's something. I know that it will be impossible to get anything else, so we'll have to take what we've got." Myrtle glanced at her watch. "And if we don't hurry right now, we're going to be late for class. As a retired teacher, that will be the end of me. Wanda, I'm very much afraid that you need a ride back, but you can't come to the class with us since you're not enrolled. There's got to be a library around here somewhere—do you want to relax in there for a while until we can take you home?"

Wanda shook her head. "Dan got one of the cars runnin' so I'm drivin' back." She pointed in the direction of a different parking lot than theirs.

Miles quickly pulled out his wallet. "Gas money?" he asked.

Myrtle suspected that Miles wanted to ensure Wanda could contact him again in case she had any further visions related to him.

Wanda shook her head again with a small smile revealing her scattered teeth. "I'm doin' okay," she insisted.

"All right, now we really *do* have to go," said Myrtle. "Class will be starting soon."

Wanda gave her an anxious look. "You don't *have* to go."

Myrtle sighed. "Wanda, I paid money to go. And I believe you about the danger, but we'll just be careful. I can't waste my money like that. I'll check back in with you later, okay?"

Myrtle and Miles hurried off as Wanda watched them go.

Miles said uneasily, "You don't suppose their cooking equipment will catch on fire or something? Or that maybe the building isn't in sound shape and it will cave in right over me?"

"I think you're being incredibly fanciful, especially since you ordinarily pooh-pooh Wanda's predictions." Myrtle's cane thumped on the sidewalk as she strode toward the Harris Building.

"Maybe it's different when the prediction is about me," said Miles in the tone of someone making an unpleasant discovery.

"I thought Wanda looked well," said Myrtle. "As opposed to a few months ago, I mean. She seemed stronger and healthier."

"I'm just glad she's given up the cigarettes. I suppose she seemed well," said Miles.

"And she seems to be doing better financially, too. She didn't ask you for a cent this time."

"Hmm." Miles sounded unconvinced.

They entered an older brick building with a steep staircase right inside the front door.

"Good thing I ate a healthy breakfast this morning," said Miles with a sigh as he started up the stairs.

The teacher was standing outside the door of the classroom. Actually, Myrtle and Miles could hear her before they saw her.

"More students coming!" cooed the voice. "This is going to be so much fun."

Myrtle and Miles rounded the corner to see a frowsy middle aged woman with heavy eyebrows, gray-streaked hair, and a kind smile.

"Louvenia," said Myrtle cordially. "Have you met Miles?"

"Sadly, I haven't," said Louvenia. She blushed and stammered. "I mean—of course, I've seen him around town. It's Bradley, so one really knows everyone else, doesn't one?"

Miles looked rather uncomfortable at the attention and the blushing. He cleared his throat. "It's nice to formally meet you, Louvenia. I hear from Myrtle that you're quite the cook. Lots of blue ribbons."

Louvenia gave a bow that was more of an abrupt bob. "Thanks for the kind words, Myrtle. I suppose, Miles, that you're learning how to cook to relieve your wife from kitchen duty sometimes?" She batted her lashes at him.

Now Miles was the one to blush. "Ah, no, actually. I'm a widower."

Myrtle was getting tired of Miles getting all the attention. "He and I are both trying to sharpen our skills. Reach the next level. You know."

Louvenia looked concerned, eyebrows drawing together alarmingly. "The recipes are assuming a certain level of expertise. It's really special occasion cooking. We'll learn some festive menus, wine and food pairing, table decoration—that sort of thing. This is an *advanced* class."

Myrtle frowned at her. "Of course. I'm well-aware of that, Louvenia. At my age, how could I be anything *but* advanced? I've had a lifetime of experience in the kitchen."

Miles made that odd, strangled noise again.

"Really," said Myrtle, "you should get that checked out by a doctor, Miles."

As Louvenia made nearly the same exact noise, Myrtle said sharply, "And you, too, Louvenia."

"Let's move inside, Myrtle, and see if we can find two seats together," said Miles hurriedly.

The large room had folding chairs in rows on one side with a long L-shaped counter at the front and on the side of one of the rows. Various ingredients were out at cooking stations. One wall held wire shelves stacked with pots and pans of all sizes. Behind the counter were a couple of different stoves, a refrigerator, and other appliances.

"I guess we start out in the chairs?" murmured Miles. "Or do we go full-force into the kitchen area?"

A loud voice behind them made them jump. "Louvenia said to sit wherever. Reckon we're starting out with a lecture."

Myrtle turned to see a large man in his late-fifties wearing red suspenders over a white shirt. He had a well-fed stomach and a long, brown beard. What was more, he looked very familiar. Myrtle frowned.

"You know, the last time I saw you Miz Clover, it was in a classroom." The large man smirked at her as he walked up to them. "As a matter of fact, I believe it was during detention."

Myrtle snapped her fingers. "Of course. Chester Struby! I thought you looked familiar."

Since Miles was looking lost, Myrtle said, "Miles, this is Chester Struby. Chester, this is Miles Bradford."

They shook hands and Miles said thoughtfully, "Your face isn't familiar, but your name is."

The man grinned, showing white teeth in his long beard. "Struby Construction. You might've seen the billboards. I own a construction company. We do mostly large commercial jobs, but I occasionally dip my hand back into single family home projects."

"That's it. The billboards." Miles pushed his glasses up his nose, studying Chester solemnly. "And you ... like to cook?"

It did seem a little incongruous. Chester Struby looked as if he could be at home in the great outdoors, or on a ranch, or perhaps in a sports event. He didn't seem particularly at ease in the kitchen.

Chester gave a booming laugh. "Can't picture it? Well, what I really like is to surprise people. I've got tons of interests and food happens to be one of them. I'm at the point of my life where I feel like I should start exploring some of these interests."

"Well, good for you," said Myrtle. "I guess I've got the same idea. Why not explore? That's what life is all about. Good to meet some fellow explorers."

She looked around the room. Besides Chester, there was a thin, dark-haired younger woman wearing all black. She had a tattoo of a hummingbird that took up much of her arm.

Chester bobbed his head at her. "That there's my niece, Hattie. I twisted her arm a little bit, but she had some free time to learn more about cooking."

Hattie turned on cue and gave Myrtle and Miles a small smile, although there wasn't much warmth in her brown eyes.

"Is this everyone?" asked Myrtle. "I somehow thought there'd be more."

Louvenia sang out from the door again, startling her. "We're waiting on another couple of students. There should be seven of us, counting myself."

Miles said under his breath, "I hope the low enrollment isn't due to the fact that the class isn't very good."

"Don't be silly, Miles. I'm excited that we have such a small class—it means that we'll have plenty of one-on-one time with Louvenia," said Myrtle.

"Oh boy," muttered Miles.

Myrtle and Miles took a seat and Louvenia bustled in, grabbing a small stack of papers. "Here, while we're waiting, if y'all could pass these around? It's a syllabus for the class. Make yourself familiar with it while you wait. Oh, and if you could fill out the form on the last page and leave it for me? I'd like to have your contact information and best way to reach you."

As Myrtle and Miles were working on the paperwork, an awkward-looking woman came in. Myrtle didn't know her well, but knew that she was a new member of Myrtle's book club, according to an email she'd gotten a month ago. She'd also taught her English decades ago. This was no coincidence since Myrtle had taught most of the town at one point. Bonnie Pendergrass. She wore thick glasses and she'd attempted to pull back her gray hair into a loose bun. Her clothes were ill-fitting and hung on her and a too-short skirt displayed knobby knees. She entered the room with a shy, anticipatory smile, but as soon as she set eyes on someone in the room, her face quickly changed and she looked completely horrified.

It almost looked as if she was looking at Miles, but Myrtle doubted that her mild-mannered friend could have caused such an intense reaction. Myrtle turned and saw Chester sitting behind Miles with a crooked grin on his face.

Bonnie quickly tried to mask her horror, but it was too late. She plopped down into the nearest chair, shoulders rising and falling rapidly as she tried to slow down her breathing.

Miles gave Myrtle a questioning look and Myrtle gave him a quick shrug. Louvenia sang out, "And now we have our last arriving student! We can go ahead and get started."

The last arriving student was a well-known figure in the small town: Felix Todd. His smiling face was on signs all over Bradley as he ran for mayor. As usual, he was looking crisply dressed in khaki pants and a blue button-down shirt with rolled up sleeves. The blue perfectly set off his eyes and his prematurely silver hair. He came over to embrace Myrtle, which startled her. "Mrs. Clover! My English teacher! What a pleasure to be in a classroom with *you* again." Myrtle gave him a tight smile. Ever the politician, Felix quickly shook everyone's hand, smiling and looking intently in each person's eyes, before sitting down.

Louvenia was busily picking up the completed paperwork and handing blank copies out to the latecomers. She gave Miles a simpering smile as she picked his up and he shifted uncomfortably in his seat.

"I'm so excited to get started with our cooking class! I'm sure we'll all learn a lot. I love teaching this course because every time I do, *I* learn something new, as well! We'll jump right into cooking very shortly, but first there are a few things I must go over—kitchen safety and college and classroom rules and regulations," said Louvenia.

Miles gave a small groan and Myrtle hissed at him, "Exactly as it should be!"

Chapter Three

The next forty-five minutes covered cooking safety and cooking and culinary equipment vocabulary terms. Although Louvenia unquestionably knew her material, Myrtle decided that she was a quite garrulous teacher. She'd take ten words to say something that could be easily expressed in five. Myrtle was positive that when Myrtle had been teaching, she was always very succinct and to the point. The only times Myrtle waxed poetic was over *poetry*.

Finally, it was time to cook. Louvenia seemed determined to make the students mix and mingle. "I'm going to choose partners for today. We're going to take time to switch out a couple of times, too. That way we'll get to know each other better and will also experience different cooking styles and methods. After all, at our ages, we're bringing a lot of life and cooking experience into the classroom!"

No one seemed thrilled about the idea of partners. Except, perhaps, for Miles. Myrtle narrowed her eyes to look at him. He acted as if he wanted to have the chance to partner with someone else.

Louvenia paired Myrtle with Chester, her former student wearing the suspenders. Miles was paired with Hattie, who gave him a tight smile that once again didn't reach her eyes.

The long counter became a food preparation area. Miles cast a concerned eye at the section that he and Hattie shared. He cleared his throat. "Are there any wipes, by any chance?"

"Wipes?" asked Louvenia, as if this were a cooking tool that she was unfamiliar with.

"Yes. To sanitize the area a bit more," said Miles.

Myrtle decided that Hattie had a real gift for eye-rolling.

Fortunately, there were antiseptic wipes under the kitchen sink and Miles quickly got the prep area closer to his rather exacting expectations. He mouthed at Myrtle: *danger*. Apparently, he thought germs and bacteria could possibly be the threats Wanda warned him about.

Chester laughed. "I reckon our area is clean enough, wouldn't you say, Miz Clover?"

They listened to the instructions for a few minutes and then Myrtle and Chester started chopping vegetables.

Myrtle said, "I was teasing with Miles before coming here that we'd probably know everyone in the class since it's such a small town. But actually, I only know a couple."

Chester snorted. "You're lucky then." He expertly diced a carrot.

Myrtle frowned. Her tomatoes didn't want to be chopped as well as Chester's carrot did. "You mean that you know more people here?"

"I know *everyone* here," said Chester lightly. And in the same light voice he said, "And I think a few of them might like to kill me. Heck, I even recognized the janitor on the way into the classroom."

Myrtle made a face at the tomato, which was now bludgeoned beyond recognition. She had the feeling that Chester was putting her on a little. She resurrected a long-ago memory of Chester coming up with tall tales in school—the kinds of tales that made teenage boys want to be like him. Some things didn't change.

Louvenia sang out, "How are we coming along?" She grimaced when she saw the obliterated tomato. "Would you like to try again with an onion, maybe, Myrtle?"

Myrtle did *not* want to try again with an onion. The only reason the tomato was in the shape it was in was because Chester had distracted her, which was most annoying. "How about if I simply get another tomato?" Myrtle made an attempt at a reassuring smile. "I'll pay more attention this time."

Louvenia's brow crinkled doubtfully, but she did sacrifice another tomato. "We're just a little low on tomatoes, that's all."

"I'll treat it with care," vowed Myrtle.

As soon as Louvenia wandered away, Myrtle started in on the tomato with a vengeance. She would *not* allow her cooking skills to be defined by a wayward tomato.

It stuck in her craw a bit that Chester was being such a braggart about being a tough guy. She decided to challenge him on it.

"Now Chester, what on earth makes you think that everyone here wants to kill you?" Myrtle heard the sour note in her voice and tried to make herself sound sweeter. "I mean, you certainly seem nice enough. And I don't remember that you were a particularly polarizing figure back in high school. As I recall, you were a football player."

Chester guffawed, making Miles turn to look curiously at them from several stations away. "Listen to you, Miz Clover! Once an English teacher, always an English teacher. I might just have to pull my pocket dictionary to look up polar ...well, whatever it was that you said."

"Don't be silly. You know it perfectly well in the context of the sentence," said Myrtle with even more irritation. Apparently, spending time with Chester was transporting her back to her classroom. Or rather, her classroom on a bad day.

He stared at her between narrowed eyes and Myrtle returned the stare until he gave another gruff laugh. "Okay. Tell you what—you agree to stop pulverizing that tomato and I'll tell you some of the lies the other students have concocted about me." He stopped and looked pleased. "Well, I'll be doggoned. Maybe being around you is a good influence, Miz Clover. I just used a couple of ten dollar words, myself!"

Myrtle looked down at her tomato. Sadly, it had been nearly converted to tomato paste again. Perhaps Chester had salvaged it, however. It simply didn't do to get distracted in here.

Louvenia sailed over again briefly. "Chester, since you're doing such a *lovely* job of chopping, I'm going to give you more vegetables to chop up for us for other recipes. Here are some baggies, too." She gave him a pleased smile which was met by a grunt.

Louvenia glanced at Myrtle's chopping board and sighed. "Oh dear."

Myrtle straightened to her formidable full height of slightly below six feet. "The tomato will taste the same."

"I suppose so," conceded Louvenia. She sighed and hurried off again.

"Our teacher," growled Chester. "She's not what she appears. If I'd have known she was in charge of this class, I wouldn't be here right now. Them college catalogs don't show who the teacher is sometimes, just the class description."

Myrtle flinched at the incorrect use of *them*. Clearly, Chester needed to have paid more attention in her class. "You're saying that Louvenia is one of the people who would like to kill you? That seems farfetched. The woman just praised your chopping skills and gave you more to dice." A fact which rankled her.

"She's a nasty person, believe me. And be sure not to tell her *anything*. Even if you *don't* tell her anything, she'll probably still figure out your deepest, darkest secret." He gave a dry laugh. "And them others—like I said—even the janitor cleaning up down the hall? I know 'em all."

Myrtle said briskly, "Well, as I was telling Miles when we came in, we should know everyone in the class. Bradley isn't exactly a metropolis. You're not even the only person I've taught in here."

She had realized immediately that she'd taught Bonnie. And naturally she'd taught Felix, as well. Chester's niece, Hattie, was far too young for her to have taught, however.

Chester snorted. "Well, I know you taught Bonnie Pendergrass, because she and I was in the same class."

Myrtle resisted the urge to call Chester out on his outlandish use of *was*, deciding instead to focus on Bonnie. She did have some faint recollections of Bonnie and Chester involving after school detention. Although she had the feeling that it was Chester who was in ASD and not Bonnie.

They were interrupted by Louvenia's high voice. "Class? Okay, now all our ingredients are chopped up and we're ready to put them in our different dishes. Hattie has the pasta cooked and ready to go."

Hattie's disinterested gaze studied the inside of the pot. "I guess it's al fresco."

Myrtle rolled her eyes. But at least this was a misuse of Italian and not English. Miles mouthed *al dente* to himself as if he was barely refraining from making a comment.

But Louvenia was either in too much of a hurry or too distracted to notice and didn't correct Hattie.

"Everyone ready?" she sang out. "Let's cook!"

When cooking class wrapped up for the day, Myrtle and Miles carefully descended the steep stairs and left the building.

"Well, that was interesting," said Myrtle.

"Not the word that *I'd* have used. I already knew how to chop vegetables. And I think Louvenia was being very persnickety about how she wanted the chopping done. I suppose the finished meal was attractive. I didn't eat it, of course, since I'm in danger and everything." Miles shivered.

"You were silly about refusing the food. It tasted fine. Besides, Wanda mentioned nothing about the entire class being wiped out by a vegetarian casserole. I do agree with you about the pickiness of our instructor. My tomatoes were perfectly fine. But I mean—that *Chester* was interesting."

"Was he?" asked Miles doubtfully. "He seemed like he might be rather crass to me. And rather unkempt. I just didn't get a very good feeling about him. He was … shifty. I wouldn't want to have him do any construction work for me." He suddenly swung around fearfully as if Chester might be lurking in the shadows behind him, waiting to catch him making a derogatory statement.

"I don't know about him being shifty, but I do think he might have a persecution complex of some kind. He seemed to think that everyone in that classroom was out to get him. Maybe it's just that he had a big ego," said Myrtle as they walked outside.

"Including you and me?" asked Miles in alarm.

"No. Just everyone else, the teacher included."

Miles said glumly, "I suppose he and I will end up as partners sometime soon. Heaven forbid." He stopped short and squinted ahead of them. "Is that *Wanda* over there? All these hours later?"

"It can't be," said Myrtle.

But it was. Her scrawny figure perched on a bench, foot swinging, patiently waiting for them to notice her.

"Class over?" she asked in her gruff voice.

"It is. But why are you still here, Wanda?" Myrtle sat down next to her on the bench.

"Car won't start," said Wanda with a heavy sigh.

"Little wonder," muttered Miles. All of the cars in Wanda's yard were either up on concrete blocks, were *about* to be up on concrete blocks, or *should* be up on concrete blocks. None of them were what an ordinary person would deem roadworthy.

"I'm sure Miles can take a look at it for you," said Myrtle.

"Me?" Miles stared at her.

"You're always so fond of telling me that you were an engineer," said Myrtle. "So take a look and see what's wrong with the thing."

"I wasn't an *automotive* engineer," said Miles coldly.

"Whatever. You should have enough experience to look under a hood," said Myrtle.

Miles sighed. "Where is your car, Wanda?"

Wanda stood up and pointed a long, thin arm to a location that was fairly far away. "Yonder."

Wanda and Myrtle watched as Miles stalked away.

"How was the class?" asked Wanda, face wrinkled in concern.

"Oh, it was okay. The teacher was a little annoying and our classmates weren't really what I expected. And I don't think I learned anything today that I can use for my dinner party," said Myrtle.

Wanda intoned, "*A crust eaten in peace is better than a banquet partaken in anxiety.*"

"Yes, yes, I know all about that. You were talking about it earlier, remember? I don't know why everyone is so against my having a dinner party." Myrtle paused and tilted her head slightly. "What on earth is Miles doing? He's already walking back. Did he even put the hood up?"

Wanda shifted on the bench. "Sure could use a smoke," she said.

"No, you couldn't. You know how horrible smoking is for you—and I'm very proud of you for quitting. Here, have some water instead." Myrtle whipped out a small water bottle from her voluminous purse.

Wanda gave her a wry look. "Ain't quite the same."

"It certainly isn't. Which is exactly the point." Myrtle thrust the bottle at her and then stood up. "Miles! I meant for you to look under the hood of the car. How else could you diagnose its problem?"

Miles said, "Very simply. The car is out of gas."

Wanda reddened a bit. "Hmm."

Miles gave her a sharp look.

"Well, we'll simply have to drive home, get a gas can, fill it up, and then give Wanda's car enough to get her back home," said Myrtle.

"*I* don't have a gas can at home. That is, I do, but it's gas mixed with oil to power the weed trimmer. And I'm assuming that *you* don't have a gas can since you: A. Don't have a car, and B. Have a yardman who brings his own equipment." Miles was already fishing in his pants for his cell phone. He pulled it out and stared dully at it. "We should call Red and see if he can help us, but my phone battery is dead. Can you call?"

Myrtle clucked and dove into her purse again for her own phone. "For heaven's sake. I left my phone at home."

They looked at Wanda, who had a very basic phone for her horoscope-writing work at the newspaper. She shook her head. "Don't carry it around with me."

"Let's head back into the school and use their phone to call Red," said Miles, already starting to trudge in that direction.

Myrtle said, "We have a dead car and a dead phone!"

Wanda said laconically, "That ain't all that's dead."

Miles and Myrtle stared dumbly at Wanda.

"Are you suggesting that there is a corpse in the cooking class?" asked Myrtle, studying Wanda between narrowed eyes.

"I'm saying that you may as well go ahead and get Red heading in this direction," said Wanda calmly.

Miles now looked even less enthused than he did before about helping out with the growing list of problems. "Why don't you come in with us, Wanda?"

Wanda shook her head. "Don't like the dead. They sometimes speak to me."

Myrtle said impatiently, "Maybe we want to hear what they have to *say* sometimes! Who is it?"

But even as she asked the question, she felt she must know the answer. It had to be Chester, of course. Who else? He was the one who thought everyone was out to get him. She'd thought he had an incredible ego, but what if he was right?

"Let's go," said Miles with a sigh. Every step he took toward the building was leaden with reluctant resolve.

Wanda sat on her bench, blinking impassively, watching them as they walked away.

"When I retired," said Miles, now slightly out of breath on the stairs, "I envisioned this quiet, peaceful life in the pastoral setting of Bradley. I'd read books; I'd spend time gazing at the lake."

"Which you do," said Myrtle, using her cane to help move her up the steep stairs like a mountain climber. "You read books all the time. You even belong to a book club." Here she couldn't help but snicker a bit. The book club selections were hardly literary, no matter how hard Myrtle and Miles tried to influence the other members.

Miles gave her a cold look at the snicker. "Perhaps I read, but I don't think I've got the entire package I was picturing. Instead, I seem to be spending a good deal of time hanging out with someone who consistently discovers dead bodies."

"You act as though that's a personal failing. I'm actually helping to promote the cause of justice. We're noble, you and I."

Miles grumbled the rest of the way up the stairs.

When they reached the top of the stairs, Miles stopped short. "It certainly is quiet up here. I don't think anyone else is still here. In fact, I'm not remembering a telephone in the classroom at all. Perhaps we should try to find an administrative office, instead."

"I think every classroom has a landline somewhere. Besides, Wanda told us that something is wrong here. It's our civic duty to check it out." Myrtle pushed ahead, cane clacking on the old tile floor.

Miles followed reluctantly behind.

They heard a piercing scream, which made Myrtle walk even faster ahead. "That sounded like Louvenia!"

"How could you tell?" gasped Miles. "From a scream?"

But it was indeed Louvenia. She started as they approached her and then her shoulders sank in relief when she saw who it was. She pointed wordlessly into the classroom, clutching Miles for protection.

"Shall I call the police?" asked Miles, looking longingly toward the staircase.

Myrtle was already moving into the classroom. She paused when she saw the large body of Chester on the floor, a digital meat thermometer extending from the side of his neck, eyes staring blankly at the ceiling.

"He's finished," she said grimly.

Chapter Four

Myrtle said in a calm voice, "I can see that there actually isn't a phone in the classroom Miles, so if you wouldn't mind finding one?"

Miles, looking a little gray, disengaged himself from Louvenia and hurried off to find one.

Myrtle carefully entered the room to take the chance to find any clues she could by the time that Red arrived and shooed her away from the crime scene.

"Do you think you should go in there?" clucked Louvenia. "I mean, if we do, won't we leave evidence in there? Our DNA or something?"

"Pooh, Louvenia. We've left our DNA all over the place in here already—we were eating and drinking and cooking and carrying on all day long. That's why it was such a great place for the murderer to kill Chester." Myrtle walked as close to Chester as she dared to go. She *did* know that she wasn't supposed to mess with a body.

She could see that there appeared to be no fight whatsoever. There weren't signs of any bruises or cuts on Chester or any other sign of violence that she could see. And Chester, with his burly, outdoorsy build, could certainly have put up a fight if he were expecting one. It would appear that, despite his understanding that people in the classroom weren't fans of his, he hadn't been expecting the blow that killed him.

Louvenia was still making lots of nervous sounds, but was now walking into the room, herself, and heading rather swiftly to her desk in the corner. She was rustling through papers and chattering as she went: "To think we were all just in here! And someone came in off the street and killed this poor man!"

Myrtle scoffed. "That's extremely unlikely, isn't it? It's a lot more likely that someone here in this class did it. It's not as if the classroom was robbed."

Everything in the classroom appeared to be exactly where it was before. All except for the meat thermometer, that is.

Louvenia stopped rustling through her papers and walked away from her desk, holding a few. "I can't imagine that anyone in the class would have killed him."

"Can't you? Chester himself was telling me that he knew everyone in the class," said Myrtle.

Louvenia squeaked. "But that's only because Bradley is such a small town! Everyone knows everyone else. Besides, he was in construction and you couldn't get away from his television commercials or his face on the billboard." She said this last in a voice that expressed how distasteful she found his ads.

"There's nothing wrong with trying to brand yourself or your business. That's being smart. And it wasn't just that this is a small town, either. Chester told me that he had a real history with the other classmates and that he felt they were out to get him. Even you," said Myrtle, turning away from Chester to face Louvenia.

"Me? But how would I know Chester? I don't work in construction." Louvenia's eyes were huge.

"Don't you?" Myrtle's eyes narrowed. "I've known you for a while, Louvenia, and while I mostly think of you in terms of winning the peach cobbler contest at the fair, I also seem to remember that you were someone's secretary."

"*Office administrator*," corrected Louvenia, stoutly before she blushed. "And what of it?"

"Did you work for Chester?" asked Myrtle.

Louvenia hesitated and Myrtle said in a stern voice, "That's not something you should lie about, you know. It can be easily checked."

"I don't work for him *now*, as a matter of fact. I only used to. And now, if you'll excuse me, it's been a long day of teaching and this has been very upsetting. I'm going to leave and put my feet up." Louvenia started to move past Myrtle.

Myrtle lifted up her cane and blocked her way.

"You certainly are *not* leaving. You're at a crime scene," said Myrtle.

Louvenia gasped and Myrtle said, "Did you think that Chester stabbed *himself* with the meat thermometer? Hardly. You're not only at a crime scene, you discovered the body. What's more, it's your classroom. Even worse, you came into the room and are trying to leave with something that could be evidence."

"What? No!" Louvenia flushed even more and pushed back at Myrtle's cane. In the process, the flustered Louvenia dropped her papers.

She was just bending down to try to pick them up when Myrtle put her cane on top of the stack. "Nothing needs to leave this room."

"But these are *mine*!" Louvenia stooped to pull at the papers.

Louvenia spun around as Miles's tired voice came from behind him. "Red is on the way." And then, "What's going on?"

Myrtle said with a sniff, "Louvenia here is trying to remove potential evidence from a crime scene."

"I'm not! I wouldn't ever!" Louvenia spluttered.

Miles walked over, carefully averting his eyes from Chester's body. He stooped and picked up the papers from under Myrtle's cane, handing them to her.

Myrtle took them, smugly. "Thanks. And sorry, Louvenia, but rules are rules." She peered at them. "What's this? It certainly looks like a picture of some of the books at Chester's construction company. So, you *did* work there."

"I told you that I used to work there. And what if I did?" demanded Louvenia. "He's had plenty of people working for him—it's a big company and he has branches in other towns, too. Even the janitor here has worked for him in the past."

"Yes, but the difference between the janitor and you is that you have what appears to be incriminating evidence in your possession." Myrtle waved the papers in the air.

Miles carefully took the papers away from Myrtle. "I want to take a look at these, but I want to do it *out* of this classroom. What will Red say if we're all standing around in here while a dead body is just feet away?" He shivered and led the way out of the room.

They followed him out, Louvenia with her tiny, mincing steps and Myrtle moving slowly out, casting looks behind her at the classroom.

Miles pushed his glasses up his nose and studied the papers. He raised his eyebrows and looked up at Louvenia. "It appears there are some discrepancies in the books. And I'm assuming that those discrepancies correspond to this paper that lists, dates, and highlights successful bids for construction projects for Chester's company."

Louvenia gave a little shriek and then a somewhat hysterical laugh. "As a bookkeeper, I could hardly ignore such a thing, could I? I felt the need to point out the problem."

"Can you lay out exactly *what* the problem is, for those of us who aren't holding the papers?" asked Myrtle impatiently.

Miles answered for her. "The fact that Chester appeared to be paying out significant amounts of cash at the same time that his construction company won bids for projects. Pay to play, I suppose."

"A dirty way of doing business!" said Louvenia with dignity.

"And you felt compelled to enter into the equally dirty business of blackmailing," noted Myrtle.

Louvenia snapped her thin lips shut to think about this for a second or two. Then she responded, "I was merely trying to get Chester to follow the straight and narrow path. To see the error of his ways."

Miles said, "Isn't that what the police are for? Shouldn't you have gone to the police with this information, then?"

Myrtle gave Miles an approving smile. He was doing well, for a sidekick.

Louvenia bit her lip and gave them a piteous look, eyes welling with tears, hands outstretched. "You've got to understand. He didn't want me to go to the police."

"I'm sure he didn't," muttered Miles.

"We came up with … an arrangement. It was an arrangement that benefitted us both. I received some much-needed money.

He received my assurances that I wouldn't be going to the authorities about this issue," said Louvenia.

"What on earth were you going to do with the money? I seem to remember you live in the same house you grew up in. You couldn't have many expenses." Myrtle glanced at Louvenia's clothing. She was hardly buying designer duds.

Louvenia said eagerly, "I want to open a restaurant. I'm a wonderful cook—everyone says so. That way I could cook to my heart's content, plan out the décor, and really enjoy what I'd be doing. Chester even said that he'd build me a place. I was thinking about creating something really intimate—candlelight, comfy chairs, white table cloths on the tables—that sort of thing."

Myrtle and Miles exchanged glances. Louvenia seemed to be living in Fantasyland about the restaurant and didn't seem to realize the fact that her actions weren't exactly legal. Blackmail was a serious crime. She wondered what Red would say. He must be getting very close by now, even as far out as the school was.

Red was sure to put a stop to her investigating, so Myrtle quickly said, "What I don't understand is the timing of all this. Chester said that he didn't know that you were going to be here today. He didn't realize you taught the class and that he wouldn't have taken the class at all if he'd known you were going to be here."

Louvenia's mouth twisted. "That wasn't very nice of him to say. Especially since we were going to be building a restaurant together."

Miles rolled his eyes at Myrtle. Louvenia did seem to be a bit out of touch with reality.

"Anyway, clearly you brought your evidence against him to class today. But haven't you been blackmailing him for a while? Otherwise, why would Chester have had that negative reaction to seeing you here?" asked Myrtle.

Louvenia flinched at the word *blackmail* as if it hadn't really occurred to her exactly what she'd been doing. "It was more like persuasion than ... you know. And our arrangement had been going on for the last month or so. Everything was just fine. I'd started looking for a location for my restaurant. I was so excited about this cooking class so that I could tell everyone that I was going to be opening a restaurant and to look out for it."

Miles said, "I'm guessing that Chester suddenly decided that he didn't want to pay up anymore."

"He certainly didn't look like the kind of man who would allow himself to be pushed around," murmured Myrtle, glancing back into the room at his burly physique, beard, and suspenders.

Louvenia said, "He decided to stop paying me, yes, even though we had an agreement! He said that he just didn't care anymore. 'Go ahead and leak it' he said, with a shrug and a laugh. He told me that he couldn't live his life that way. But then he was forcing me to live *my* life a way that I didn't want to. He was forcing me to give up on my dream."

"You knew he was signed up for this class, though," said Myrtle, giving Louvenia a look through narrowed eyes. "You decided to bring the evidence you had against him with you today."

Louvenia gave a shrill laugh. "Why not? What did I have to lose? I wanted to remind him of everything that I knew."

Miles cleared his throat. "Although he already knew the evidence you had."

"And he'd already made up his mind," said Myrtle. "He didn't want to pay you. Your dreams went up in smoke and you saw red and killed him."

Louvenia's eyes opened wide. "No, no no! Why would I do that? He was going to build my restaurant. He was going to keep paying me, I know it! Why would I kill my money cow? No!"

"Then who *did* kill him? Any ideas? Because it had to have been someone in this classroom," said Myrtle sternly.

This time Louvenia didn't automatically defend her students. She paused for a second to think. Myrtle shifted uncomfortably and Miles raised his eyebrows at her as the sound of a siren approached.

"I know that Felix Todd was at the construction company sometimes." Louvenia reached into the classroom and pulled the closest chair out into the hall and sat down heavily in it.

"Would you like a chair?" Miles asked courteously of Myrtle.

She shook her head impatiently, still trying to focus on Louvenia's thought process. Myrtle considered Felix's entrance into the classroom today. He was all confidence, all smiles. His prematurely white hair was perfectly combed. It was hard to picture him successfully hiding a murder plot. "You mean because he's political, I suppose?"

Louvenia nodded. "If it was someone in the class, why not him? He'd call Chester sometimes and I'd be taking messages. It did seem as if something crooked was going on between the two of them. It makes the most sense, as far as I can tell. I'm just saying that it might be something for your son to check out."

A son who was approaching quickly. She could hear the door open downstairs and footsteps entering. And then: "Mama? Where are you?" came the exasperated voice.

Louvenia looked relieved. "He's here!"

"We're upstairs and to the right," called Myrtle.

The footsteps gathered speed, jogging up the stairs. A minute later, Red was there. They pointed into the classroom. He slipped some booties on his feet and carefully entered, approaching Chester.

"All right. Now y'all need to get farther away than you are now. Is there another unlocked classroom in this building where you can sit for a while?" asked Red, still studying Chester and now crouched next to him.

Louvenia considered this. "All the classrooms are supposed to be locked when no one is here. And I don't have a key to the faculty lounge since I'm just a part-time instructor here. But I can find the custodian, Amos. I've seen him around on and off today. He can open a classroom for us."

Louvenia went scurrying off to find the custodian. Red said, "I've called the state police. I'm just confirming Chester is deceased, securing the scene, and making a few notes." He looked up grimly at his mother. "I knew you were going to be taking a class today, but I hardly expected a body to crop up. What's this all about?"

Myrtle tried to keep a smug smile from tugging at the corners of her lips. She always liked it when Red was the one to ask *her* the questions. "I might have an *inkling* of what's going on. Chester and I were class partners today, you see."

Red turned back around to study Chester. "I'd assume he was poisoned then, except for this meat thermometer sticking out of his neck."

"Ha, ha, ha." Myrtle put her hands on her hips.

Miles cleared his throat. "The entire class contributed to the food we prepared today. I think that was a 'beginner level' thing."

"Which doesn't even matter, since he clearly *wasn't* poisoned, by me or by anyone else," said Myrtle with irritation. "And stop pretending that you know anything about this. You were too busy sanitizing your workspace to do any detecting."

Miles said coldly, "There wasn't any detecting to *do* at the time." He said to Red in a whisper, "But there was a bit of detecting afterwards. And you should spend some time talking to Louvenia." He gestured down the hall.

Myrtle gave him a furious look. It was very annoying for sidekicks to give information to the local police.

"Thanks for the information, Miles," said Red. "How about one more tidbit? Time of death?"

Myrtle said, "It must be a very narrow window. The class was over at two o'clock. Miles and I left pretty quickly, but then we were held up." She gasped and looked over at Miles.

Miles nodded. "I totally forgot."

"Can one of y'all fill me in?" asked Red.

Myrtle said, "Well, Wanda showed up."

"*Wanda*? What was she doing out here? Surely she's not enrolled in school." Red's face was incredulous.

"No, no, nothing like that. Wanda was here to deliver a cryptic message. At any rate, when Miles and I were leaving, we were shocked to see that Wanda was still here. I mean, we'd last seen her early this morning. She had car trouble and Miles was unable to fix the vehicle." Myrtle waved her hand in an airy gesture at Miles.

Miles said stiffly, "It wasn't 'car trouble.' The car was out of gas. At any rate, I was going back into the building to call you, Red. I wanted to see if you could get a gas can filled so that we could help Wanda leave."

Red groaned. "So, I've also got a psychic stranded motorist here to help."

"Well, at this point, I think Miles can just go find a gas station, purchase a gas can, fill it up, and deposit it in Wanda's tank. We simply thought you might be patrolling in the area and could quickly help us out. But having a body here changes everything." Myrtle paused. "Wanda told us about the body, you know."

Red's eyes narrowed. "Wanda was in here?"

"No, she was either out of the classroom or with us the whole time. But she has *powers* and that's how she knew about Chester. Anyway, that was another reason we figured we were going to have to call you," said Myrtle.

Red sighed. "I think I'll just keep Wanda's knowledge of Chester's death to myself for now. I don't think the state police will have the same take on it that you do, Mama."

Myrtle sniffed. "Maybe they need to open their minds a little."

An out-of-breath Louvenia appeared. "Amos is opening up a classroom for us a few doors down." She fluttered her eyelashes at Miles and he stiffened.

"Excellent. The state police should be here shortly. I'd appreciate y'all staying in the classroom until we have a chance to get statements."

"What about Wanda?" demanded Myrtle.

"All right. Mama, you can go down and tell Wanda what's going on. Let her know it might be another hour until you can get her car filled up." Red shook his head. "What a day."

Chapter Five

Louvenia and Miles headed off to the classroom (Miles trudging away reluctantly) and Myrtle hurried off to see Wanda. She was now curled up on the bench and appeared to be sleeping.

Myrtle put a hand on her shoulder and gently patted her. "Wanda?"

Wanda stirred and sat slowly up. "Find the dead man?"

"We did. And we've been dealing with the ramifications of finding him ever since, which is why this is taking so long. Red says it'll be another hour before we can leave and get your car gassed up." Myrtle hesitated. "Are you hungry?"

Wanda was always hungry. "Been a while since breakfast."

Myrtle slid her purse off her shoulder and rummaged through it. "All I've got in here are peppermints." She glanced around. "That looks like a coffee shop over there. They should at least have muffins or something." She carefully pulled out a few bills from her wallet and handed them to Wanda.

"Thanks," said Wanda, quickly taking the money.

Myrtle said, "You sure you didn't have any other thoughts about the dead man?"

Wanda shook her head. "The sight don't...."

"I know, I know. The sight doesn't work that way. I've got to get back. See you in about an hour," said Myrtle, hurrying away again, cane hitting the cement pathway with heavy thumps.

When Myrtle made it back to the holding classroom, she saw an anxious and stressed Miles and a now-tearful Louvenia.

"This is terrible, awful," Louvenia moaned. She sniffed loudly.

Miles cleared his throat, shifting uncomfortably on his feet. "The classroom doesn't' seem to be equipped with tissues."

"We're not *imprisoned* in the classroom, you know. It's fine for us to leave and visit the restroom for a tissue!" said Myrtle.

Miles didn't move. "Red didn't *say* it was all right to leave."

Miles was not a rule-breaker, particularly where the police were concerned.

Louvenia, though, with a strangled sob, stumbled from the classroom in the direction of the restroom.

Miles's shoulders slumped with relief. "Thank heaven you're back. She's been driving me crazy."

Myrtle frowned. "Surely she's not pretending to be grieving Chester. That would be disingenuous of her."

"I don't think she even disliked Chester. She simply looked at what she was doing as a business transaction. Louvenia kept quiet about Chester's underhanded dealings with the local government and Chester paid her. I think she was grieving the loss of her *restaurant*, mainly." Miles rubbed his forehead. "And frankly, all of her sobbing and gnashing of teeth, not to mention the flirting, is giving me a terrible headache. Do you have any ibuprofen or anything?"

Myrtle reached once again into her voluminous pocket-book, retrieving a couple of small pills and a water bottle. "Here."

Miles took the medicine, washing it down with much of the water bottle. He eyed Myrtle's bag. "I'm shocked you didn't have any tissues in that purse of yours."

"Oh, I do," said Myrtle coolly. "I was just trying to rid us of the scourge of the hysterical Louvenia for a few minutes."

"Smart." Miles sat gingerly down in a small desk. "What did you make of Louvenia's story?"

"I'm wondering if she got angry enough with Chester to kill him in a rage. She sure seemed sold on that restaurant of hers. Maybe she thought that she was just going to threaten him into giving her money again, but lost control and stabbed him."

Myrtle paused as a man in his thirties wearing a blue denim shirt and old khakis stuck his head through the door. He had a large keychain with many keys hanging on a brown belt.

"Everything okay in here?" he asked.

"For now, yes. You must be Amos, the custodian," said Myrtle.

"Yes ma'am." He gave them a curious look. "You must have found ... him?"

"The body?" asked Myrtle briskly. "That's correct."

Amos shook his head. "Well, it's a pity." His unemotional eyes belied his words.

"You knew him, then?" asked Miles.

"Used to work for him," said Amos, leaning against the door jamb.

Myrtle said, "You were a construction worker for him or in the office?"

Amos gave a short laugh. "Would've been better if I'd been in the office. No, I was out there at the sites, climbing up on scaffolding and doing all sorts of stuff for him. It paid pretty well, too. That was really the problem—I got used to how great the pay was. I stopped renting and bought a house. Then I got married."

"I presume that there's a twist in this nice story," said Myrtle. "An accident, perhaps?"

Amos patted his leg and his back. "You got it. I got hurt on the job and that was the end of construction for me. I just couldn't handle the work anymore. At least, I was so slow that no one would hire me. That's how I ended up as a custodian."

Miles frowned. "But surely you'd have had workman's compensation?"

"Or disability?" asked Myrtle.

Amos shook his head. "Afraid not. I was a contract worker, you see. I got more money that way because Chester didn't have to pay me any insurance or any other benefits."

Myrtle's eyes opened wide. "No insurance? But your hospital bills ....?"

"They were pretty bad, especially with no money coming in. I lost my house and my wife left me. Now I'm back to renting again and living alone. But the college treats me decent," added Amos, as an afterthought.

"You seem awfully well-adjusted about this turn of events, Amos. You're not bitter about it?" asked Myrtle.

He gave another short laugh. "Well, everything happens for a reason, doesn't it? I'm one to let bygones be bygones. Life's too short, isn't it? I mean ... look what happened to Chester."

"Yes, Chester," said Myrtle. "About that—you didn't happen to be around to see or hear anything unusual, did you?"

Amos turned slightly toward the sound of voices down the hall. The state police appeared to have arrived. He turned back to Myrtle and said, "I don't know exactly when it happened, of course. But at the end of the class I was refilling the soap dispensers and replacing a couple of lightbulbs."

It wasn't much of an alibi, but he didn't seem to consider himself a suspect for some reason. Chester had mentioned knowing Amos, though, and had made a fairly blanket statement about being unpopular with everyone.

"You didn't see anyone?" asked Miles, pushing his glasses up his nose.

"I saw Louvenia," he said, tilting his head in the direction of the hall.

"Yes, of course you did," said Myrtle with a sigh. "She was in charge of the class. I suppose you saw a lot of students, too."

"Yes, but I mean that I saw her acting sort of odd when I was mopping the floor downstairs, after changing out the lightbulbs. She didn't see me, but she came running down the stairs, stopped, muttered to herself, and then hurried back up them again. She acted almost afraid the first time she came down."

"This was *before* she started screaming?" asked Miles.

Amos nodded.

"So, she might have seen the body before she started *screaming* at the body," said Myrtle.

Miles said under his breath, "Or perhaps she simply sampled some of the students' cooking. I have a feeling that some of the cooking might have caused that reaction."

"Don't be facetious," said Myrtle.

Amos said, "It was before any screaming, that's for sure."

Myrtle gave him a sharp look. "You heard Louvenia screaming? Then why didn't you come?"

Amos flushed. "I didn't hear any screaming. But I had lots of water running to wash out my mop bucket. I just mean that it must have been *before* her screaming because y'all both joined her *after* the screaming. Right?"

Myrtle said slowly, "Right." But she could tell he was hiding something.

She didn't have time to contemplate what exactly Amos was concealing because a hassled-looking Red stuck his head through the door. "Okay," he said, "I think I can start getting some statements. Mama and Miles, I suppose I'll take you first, since you've got urgent business to attend to."

Miles looked confused at the 'urgent business', and Myrtle hissed, "Wanda!"

"And, sir, you're the custodian here?" Red asked Amos. "I'll need to speak with you, too, so if you could stay?"

He glanced around. "Where's Louvenia?"

Myrtle said, "She got herself worked up and escaped to the restroom to blow her nose."

Red said, "Can you check on her? I'll need to speak with her, too."

Myrtle made a face. "She may be dissolved in tears."

"I know that you're allergic to people crying, but I want to be sure I speak with her before she leaves," said Red with a sigh.

Amos said, "I'll go. I always pound on the restroom before I go in to clean it, anyway."

A minute later they heard him say loudly, "Custodian. May I clean?" He gave a very authoritative knock on the door.

There was apparently no answer, because he repeated himself and the knocking. Amos returned to them, shaking his head.

Red sighed again. "Really? Now I've got to go hunt Louvenia down?"

Miles said, "She likely just went home. She was in quite a state."

"She shouldn't have been driving like that," said Myrtle.

Miles said, "Maybe she went home to draft an email to everyone to cancel class tomorrow." There was a hopeful edge to his voice.

Red said, "The forensics guys from the state police will be done with it way before your class starts tomorrow."

"I'd think she'd cancel out of respect. For Chester," said Miles.

Myrtle said, "That's the whole point, though. Chester wasn't exactly highly regarded by his classmates. No, I think class will probably continue."

Miles looked glum. He looked even glummer as Red pulled Myrtle and him out to another classroom to get their statements.

To Myrtle's surprise and delight, Detective Lieutenant Perkins from the state police was the responding officer. Apparently, he'd already been in the area for a meeting of some kind.

"Lieutenant Perkins," purred Myrtle. "My favorite police officer!"

Red rolled his eyes and Myrtle added, "Aside from my son, of course. And how well you look! Crime fighting must agree with you. Or is it those daily crossword puzzles that you were telling me you did? I keep telling Red he should take up crosswords or his brain will rot. Middle age is very destructive."

Lieutenant Perkins smiled warmly at her. He did indeed look well with his clipped, military haircut and his wiry frame in neatly-pressed suit pants and a button-down white shirt with a red tie.

He answered diplomatically, "Even if I did three or four crosswords a day, I wouldn't be as sharp as you, Mrs. Clover."

Myrtle beamed at him and Red rolled his eyes again.

Finally, they were done with Red—*and* the state police, both of which had entered and asked questions during the interview. They hurried downstairs.

"This has been the longest afternoon ever," said Miles.

"If it's been that long for us, think how long it's been for poor Wanda. I wonder if she's still in the coffee shop or if she is back on that bench," said Myrtle.

Wanda was indeed back on the bench. She stood up, stretching, as they approached her.

Myrtle said, "Okay, now we're in business. Miles, you go get a gas can and fill it up. I'll be some company for Wanda until you get back."

"It might be a little while. I have no idea where any gas stations might be." Miles did not sound thrilled about his mission.

"Just use your phone," said Myrtle impatiently. "Use your phone to locate gas stations on the GPS."

"My phone is dead, remember? I'll just drive around a bit." Miles strode off.

Myrtle rolled her eyes at Wanda. "Miles does have one thing right. It's the longest afternoon ever. Sorry you've spent most of it on a bench."

Wanda shrugged a thin shoulder. "It was okay. Better than home." She snapped her fingers. "Almost forgot." She dug in an old bag she was carrying. "Here."

Wanda handed Myrtle a pile of curled up papers with scribbling on it. Apparently, they were a slew of horoscopes for Myrtle to edit before handing them to Sloan at the paper.

Myrtle sighed. Now she had a case to work on and a story to write for the newspaper. Glancing through the papers, she saw some of the horoscopes would need more decoding than others.

Wanda nodded at the papers. "Some of them is time-sensitive," she said.

Myrtle took out a pen. "Pull those out for me while we're waiting."

Wanda found one that warned Franklin Brown that coyotes were moving in on his chickens and one that told Susan Powell to avoid ladders at all costs.

Myrtle looked at Wanda curiously. "Wanda, all of my classmates are in your horoscopes."

Wanda shook her head. "Not all of 'em."

Myrtle flipped through them again. "All right. Not Chester." She gave a little shiver. "Let me see. They all seem to be warnings."

"Friendly warnings," corrected Wanda.

Myrtle decoded the scrawl and recited, "Bonnie: Open your eyes. Amos: Seize your chance. Hattie: It's a seller's market. Felix: Avoid leaving town."

Wanda shrugged.

It took another twenty-five minutes before Miles joined them again. After he put some gas in Wanda's car, she drove slowly off, the rusty old car making all kinds of terrible noises as she left.

"Let's get out of here before she has more car trouble," muttered Miles.

Myrtle climbed in and Miles started off at a much faster speed than he had driven on the way *to* school.

Myrtle said, "That Amos was hiding something."

Miles snorted. "Wouldn't you? Although he should have hidden even more than he did. It wasn't very bright of him to tell us that he'd worked for Chester and that he was injured on the job while working for him."

"It's something Red or Detective Lieutenant Perkins from the state police would have found out anyway," said Myrtle with a shrug. "Besides, the way he was acting, he wasn't bitter at all. Maybe he *likes* working on a community college campus instead of working on a construction site."

"Maybe he does. But I got the impression that he didn't like the reduction in his income," said Miles.

"Exactly. And I didn't buy his explanation about Louvenia screaming. That he was running water and couldn't hear her. I think he didn't come because he *knew* what she'd seen because he'd already seen Chester's dead body." Myrtle's eyes narrowed.

"You think Amos killed him?" asked Miles. "Even though he didn't seem bitter?"

"I don't know if he *killed* him, but I think he found the body and didn't want to get involved. And it sounds like he wasn't the only one, if what he's saying is true. He thought Louvenia found the body and was just screaming for effect."

"Found the body or *murdered* him?" asked Miles.

"I don't know. I'd have said the only thing Louvenia Defore was likely to cook up was a prize-winning pie, but she sure did seem carried away with the thought of that restaurant," said Myrtle.

Miles pulled up into Myrtle's driveway. "You said we'd watch the tape of *Tomorrow's Promise* together when we were done with class."

Tomorrow's Promise was a soap opera that Myrtle had been watching for several decades. The acting was over-the-top, the storylines were ridiculous, but she was hooked. She'd managed to get Miles hooked too: a fact he made her swear to secrecy to conceal.

"I did say that. That was when we were supposed to come home in early afternoon. I feel like we were at that school for a week. Besides, I'm going to call Sloan Jones now that I've got an exclusive," said Myrtle, opening the car door.

Sloan Jones was the editor of the *Bradley Bugle* newspaper and he and Red were friends who had gone to school with each other. Myrtle had taught Sloan decades ago.

Miles gave her a repressive look. "Myrtle, I don't think that Red will be happy about that."

"Who cares? It's a free country, the last time I checked. And it's a free press. I've got a hot lead and Sloan is going to put a big story over whatever promises he's made to Red, believe me. He's always got an eye out for making a buck."

Miles said, "You know that Red wants you to stick with writing your helpful hints column. I always hear that people love reading that stuff here."

"The popularity of the column is propaganda that Red spreads. Who wants to read about laundry tips? Bleh." Myrtle reached for her pocketbook and took it off the floor of the car.

"Just the same, I think Red is going to intervene and make sure you're writing helpful hints instead of a news exclusive," said Miles, sounding worried.

"I'll have a helpful hint for Red the next time he tries telling me what to do," said Myrtle sourly. "See you later."

She walked up her walkway, cane thumping as she went. Myrtle was deep in thought and startled when she felt something brush against her leg.

Chapter Six

"Pasha!" exclaimed Myrtle. "You about scared me half to death."

The feral black cat's eyes smiled naughtily up at her.

"Want to come in and have a snack?" asked Myrtle, as she fumbled with her keys.

She managed to quickly sidestep a love offering from Pasha that she'd laid on Myrtle's front step. Pasha seemed to think that Myrtle was hopeless at hunting and kept bringing her dead gifts as encouragement to try harder.

"I'm going to have to get Red to take care of that corpse later. I don't think Puddin will do it," muttered Myrtle to herself. She pushed open her front door and followed as Pasha strolled casually inside.

Pasha walked straight to Myrtle's kitchen, still apparently in hunting phase as she scoured the room looking for things to kill. To Myrtle's relief, as she pulled out a can of cat food, there appeared to be nothing for Pasha to assault. Soon the cat was gobbling up the cat food that Myrtle put on a paper plate.

"Now you've made me lose my train of thought," scolded Myrtle in an affectionate voice. "I was coming in here to do something, and I know it wasn't to watch my soap. Oh, that's right—Sloan."

Sloan picked up the phone immediately, although he sounded sleepy. "*Bradley Bugle*," said Sloan.

"Sloan? Myrtle Clover here."

She heard a lot of sudden squeaking in the background. Myrtle could picture him in his stuffy, dimly-lit newsroom. The squeaking must be due to Sloan trying to correct the posture of his heavy frame. His rolling desk chair sounded as if it must be going through death throes. Sloan always snapped to attention when his former teacher called.

"Miss Myrtle! Good to hear from you. I hope you've got a column for me. I was just about to email you."

"Actually, I'm calling because I've got a big story I wanted to tell you about," said Myrtle briskly. She watched as Pasha cleaned the plate of every bit of food.

Sloan groaned. "Miss Myrtle, I don't know if I can handle another big story of yours. You remember the last time you called me with a story?"

"I can't help it that this town is so boring that the only thing that qualified as a big story was the herd of deer cavorting in Darlene Kirby's yard. Actually, I have a follow-up for that story, too. It appears that Darlene was *feeding* the deer and that's why they were so interested in hanging out in her yard. I believe Darlene should have given us full disclosure on that at the very beginning. She made it sound like something mystical was happening." Myrtle sat down at her kitchen table. "And it was just corn happening."

Sloan hesitated, seeming to grope for words. "So, this isn't a deer story? Or a rabid raccoon story?"

"Not at all. It's a murder story. An *exclusive*. I happened to be there at the time," said Myrtle.

"You saw a murder?" There was more chair squeaking in the background.

"Certainly not! I found the body, that's all. I'd like to think that I'd prevent a murder from happening, if someone were attempting it right in front of me. Anyway, this isn't just a murder. It's a murder of a rather well-known person in this town—Chester Struby."

Now she appeared to have gotten Sloan's attention. "Chester? Construction Chester?"

"The very one. I've got all kinds of details and I want to be the one to write the story. And, since the murder isn't yet solved, I want to be the correspondent assigned to the story." Myrtle thought that *correspondent* sounded a lot grander than *reporter*."

"Oh, I don't know, Miss Myrtle." Sloan's voice was anxious. "You know how Red feels about you investigating crimes."

"I didn't say that I wanted to investigate it. I merely said that I wanted to report it. Those are two very different things," said Myrtle.

"But we really do need another helpful hints column from you. You just don't know how popular those are," said Sloan in a rush.

"You're right. I *don't* know how popular those are." Myrtle rolled her eyes at Pasha, who purred loudly and brushed lovingly against Myrtle's legs.

"Why, people love them. Particularly anything to do with painting a room or birdfeeders. If you don't have any ideas for hints, maybe you could scare up something about those topics. Folks come up to me the whole livelong day and tell me how much they love and appreciate those tips."

"That's funny, because people don't come up to *me* to fawn over my column. And I'm the one writing it. Anyway! You're herding me off topic, Sloan. My story has nothing to do with hints, as I was saying. Unless the hint is that Louvenia Defore's cooking class might be hazardous to your health."

Sloan's voice changed on the phone. "You're in a cooking class?"

"Everyone can use improvement, Sloan. Learning is for life! Even for those of us who've been cooking beautifully for sixty years," said Myrtle.

There was a strangled sound on the other end of the line.

Myrtle said sharply, "Sloan! It's impolite to eat and talk on the phone at the same time."

"Wasn't eating," said Sloan in a weak voice. "Go ahead. I'm listening."

"Somehow we've veered off-topic again. Back to Chester Struby's murder. There are a few bizarre details of this case," said Myrtle. She knew that Sloan was a sucker for a story that might get picked up on the wire for other newspapers.

"Really?" Sloan couldn't keep the curiosity out of this voice.

"Yes. The murder weapon was both vicious and tragic. He was killed with a digital meat thermometer," said Myrtle.

"*What*?"

"Precisely," said Myrtle. "So, this is *my* story. I'll write it up perfectly and it's sure to be picked up by other papers. You think your friendship with Red is important because he'll give you tips for stories. Instead, it's your star reporter who's giving you the hot leads."

"Yes, Miss Myrtle," said Sloan meekly.

"I'll email you the story later today. And I'll try to decipher some of Wanda's horoscopes for you on top of all that." And Myrtle hung up.

"And *now* it's time for my soap opera," she muttered to Pasha. "Pasha, want to sit in my lap and take a nap since you have a full tummy?"

Myrtle plopped down in an armchair and picked up her remote. Pasha gingerly hopped up on Myrtle's lap. She proceeded to have a bath while Myrtle pointed the remote between Pasha's ears so the signal could reach the television.

There was a short, desperate shriek outside Myrtle's front door. Myrtle calmly continued pushing buttons on her remote.

The phone rang, startling Pasha who gave Myrtle a reproachful look. "Yes? Hello?" asked Myrtle in some irritation as she hit pause on the remote.

"Mama? Good to hear you're alive." Red's voice contradicted his words.

"Of course I am. I'm far too busy to kick the bucket. Why on earth would you think otherwise?" Myrtle stroked Pasha until the black cat settled down again.

"Oh, you know, the yelling. I'm temporarily home to grab a sandwich and heard Puddin scream. Wondered if she'd walked in on a body or something," said Red. It sounded as if he were now stuffing his sandwich down his throat as quickly as he could.

At that moment, Puddin's sullen face and dumpy body maneuvered through the door. Instead of her usual pasty white skin, she was looking decidedly green. She glared at Myrtle.

"As a matter of fact, Puddin *did* walk in on a body. Courtesy of Pasha and one that I would very much like her to remove." Myrtle said the last pointedly in a stern voice.

Puddin didn't stick her tongue out, but her expression told Myrtle that she'd considered it.

Red seemed to be chewing furiously on the other end. "That's fine then. Got to run."

"Run? Wait! What about Dusty's lawnmower? My yard looks worse than Erma's and that's patently unacceptable."

Puddin stomped past her and into the kitchen.

"No time now, Mama. I'll take care of it just as soon as I can." Red hung up.

Puddin stomped past her again on the way to the door, holding some bottles close to her chest.

Myrtle said, "Now hold on there. What on earth are you doing here? And what have I told you about just letting yourself in?"

"Forgot my cleanin' supplies," said Puddin sourly.

"That's unlikely, since they're *my* cleaning supplies. Supplies that *you* aren't supposed to be using to begin with, since you're supposed to be bringing your own here each time," said Myrtle.

Puddin shrugged, keeping a watchful eye on Pasha the whole time. She didn't like the cat one bit. Pasha, in return, rolled over on her back and swatted the air with a claw as she stared at Puddin. Then Pasha leapt up on the outstretched hands of Elaine's leering gnome and stared with great hostility at Puddin.

"What *is* that thing?" asked Puddin, making a face.

"That is a cat."

Puddin said, "I mean, what's that ugly thing she's sittin' on? Don't look like your usual statues out front."

Myrtle sighed. "It's one of Elaine's creations. A restored gnome. Elaine ... did something to it."

"She sure did." Puddin gave the statue and the cat on top of it a disgusted glance. Then a cunning look passed over her face. "So, you don't want to hurt Elaine's feelings. I could break that thing. For a little money. It could be an accident."

Myrtle said, "You should break it for me gratis, considering all the nonsense that I have to put up with between you and Dusty. But enough of that. While I have you here, and while I actually have some cleaning supplies still left in my house, isn't it about time you did some work for me? I'm getting ready to have a dinner party soon."

Puddin snorted. "Can't have a dinner party with the yard lookin' like that."

"Don't I know it! But that's something that I'm working on, at least. You can work on the inside of the house and I'll handle getting the outside looking better." Myrtle hit 'play' on her remote as if everything was settled.

"Can't clean now. My back is thrown," muttered Puddin.

"Naturally. Your back throws itself out whenever work of any kind is mentioned. It has quite an allergy to any kind of labor. Fortunately, I'm aware of this and am here to help." Myrtle hit 'pause' and started to rise from her armchair, but Pasha narrowed her eyes and Myrtle sank back down. "Put those cleaning bottles down and grab that stack of papers from the top of my desk."

Puddin dropped the plastic bottles down on the floor with a series of collective thuds and slouched over to the desk. She squinted at the words on the page. "Don't have my readin' glasses on," she said.

"You don't need them. Just look at the pictures. See all the stretches that woman in the picture is doing? These are back-strengthening stretches that will help prevent any pulled muscles in the future. They're developed by real sports medicine doctors and physical therapists." Myrtle thumped the arm of the chair emphatically and Pasha moved over to sit on the offending arm so that it wouldn't happen again.

"Might hurt," stated Puddin, glaring at the happy, stretching woman in the pictures.

"Don't be silly. The only downside for you is that you'll have to figure out some other excuse to make to get out of working. Now get rid of that corpse and do an hour of honest work and then you're welcome to whatever supplies I've got lurking under my sink."

"Got things to do," muttered Puddin.

"Hardly. You spend most of your days lollygagging around. The reason your back hurts is because you spend too much time loafing on your sofa. Corpse removal, please!" Myrtle resumed her focus on the television and hit 'play' again.

"That witch-cat," snarled Puddin, glaring at the black cat.

Pasha, the witch-cat, snarled back.

Puddin stomped off out the back door as Myrtle finally started watching her show. During the opening credits and sappy theme music, Puddin stalked back by, hefting a tremendous shovel. Myrtle rolled her eyes at Pasha. Puddin could dispose of a large man with that thing. It was overkill for a shrew or mouse or whatever the tiny body was.

On the front porch, Puddin yelped the entire time as if the poor creature was returning to life and chasing her around the yard. Myrtle sighed and turned the television up louder. "Foolishness."

Myrtle determinedly focused on the TV set as Puddin brought the shovel back through, picked up a bottle of cleaning solution, spilled half the bottle on the kitchen counter, mopped Myrtle's floor, and ran the vacuum in the back of the small house.

Pasha's ears swiveled back in displeasure at the vacuum. She seemed to think that Puddin was deliberately trying to provoke her. It was a possibility. Myrtle softly stroked the cat's back, but her calming techniques proved a failure when Puddin eventually surfaced from the back, looking rather sweaty and grumpy and pushing the now-silent vacuum. Pasha, malice quivering through every muscle in her body, launched herself at Myrtle's housekeeper.

"Aaah!" shrieked Puddin, staggering to the floor, trying to peel the black cat off of her.

Myrtle stood up and pushed the vacuum's power button again. It roared to life and Pasha rapidly evacuated. Puddin struggled to her feet, eyes huge. She stammered wordlessly for a few seconds before gasping out, "Bad kitty!"

Myrtle plopped back down in her armchair and picked up the remote. "I guess I should just stop this soap opera. There have been so many distractions and so much nonsense that it's making even less sense than it usually does."

Puddin, apparently declaring her work day finished, dropped onto the sofa, still stealing glances in the direction

Pasha had run off in. "Play it for a sec just so I can catch my breath," she pleaded.

Myrtle hit play again and Puddin was immediately absorbed. That is, absorbed until she couldn't follow the storyline.

"Does Horatio really like Cynthia? I thought they was enemies." Puddin slumped down so far into the sofa that it looked as if she might end up with the dust bunnies underneath.

"No, but Cynthia slipped a love potion into his cocktail glass and now he's besotted with her," said Myrtle. "She's planning all kinds of mischief, I'll bet. And Tatiana wants to eliminate Fiona by maiming her somehow. That way, she can have Blaine all to herself."

Spoken aloud, it all sounded more ridiculous than it already was.

A few minutes later, the closing credits started streaming. Myrtle was about to shoo Puddin out so that she could get started with her newspaper article when she remembered that Puddin was actually frequently a source for information. In fact, Puddin was part of a sort of underground network of housekeepers in the greater Bradley, North Carolina area that spent much more of their time gossiping than cleaning.

"Before you go," started Myrtle pointedly, "I did have something that I wanted to ask you."

"'Bout what?" Puddin was not making any move to stand up.

"Chester Struby. I was wondering what you knew about him. Especially if you knew if anyone had a grudge against him," said Myrtle.

As usual, Puddin's entire face crinkled with the effort of deep thought. "Chester. That's the construction guy. Hateful."

"Hateful? Why?" asked Myrtle.

"Dusty tried to get a job with him. Buildin' stuff. Wouldn't hire him. Said he was lazy," spat out Puddin resentfully.

Myrtle raised her eyebrows. It sounded as if Chester was actually a good judge of character.

"But then Dusty started up his *own* business," said Puddin. She said the words 'own business' as if Dusty were an entrepreneur with an empire instead of a yardman with a broken lawnmower.

"So what you're telling me is that your husband, Dusty, had a grudge against Chester," said Myrtle with a sigh. "Can you think of anyone else? Did anybody clean for Chester? I know he had lots of money."

"Kitty Farrigan works for him. She says that her and Chester was in school together."

Myrtle rolled her eyes. "So, I probably taught Kitty Farrigan, too."

"And *both* of them was in school with Bonnie Pendergrass," said Puddin.

"I hope this is going somewhere, Puddin, and that you're not going to simply tell me every classmate that Chester had in school," said Myrtle. "Besides, I already knew about Bonnie and Chester having a problem. And I've taken note that they were both with me in class today."

Puddin tilted her head to one side as if the thought of Myrtle in class was making her head explode. "Class?"

"Cooking school."

Now Puddin's eyes opened wide. "You're in cooking school?"

"Why ever not? Goodness, what's wrong with people? Everyone acts like I can't learn things anymore," said Myrtle in irritation.

Puddin kept her lips tightly pressed together.

"Tell me more about Bonnie Pendergrass," said Myrtle. "Did Kitty give you any details?"

Puddin shrugged. "All I know is that Chester was real mean to her in school. Kitty says that Bonnie never got over it and blames Chester to this day for never being able to make anything of her life. She's always takin' them personal improvement classes. Sorta sad. Kitty never forgot it and she says she hates working for a mean man, but she needs the money."

"Well, tell Kitty that she needs to look for another job. She won't be working for a mean man any longer. Chester Struby was murdered this afternoon."

"That's terrible. Awful." Puddin's eyes gleamed with the knowledge that she had gossip that no one else had yet.

"Yes, it is. Now look—I've got things to do. What's more, *you* have things to do," said Myrtle.

"What kinds of things?" asked Puddin as she caught hold of the coffee table and dragged herself off the sofa.

"Stretching exercises. For your back, remember?"

"If I have time." Puddin stooped to collect the cleaning solution bottles. She strode with her small nose in the air toward the door. Her air of dignified resentment was utterly ruined when Pasha, hissing, jumped wildly out at her as Puddin walked by.

Myrtle supposed that Red was too far out of earshot to hear *that* scream.

Chapter Seven

Myrtle spent the rest of the day writing the news article. She read it over with satisfaction and emailed it to Sloan as promised.

Once it was done, she realized in surprise that she was sleepy. Myrtle rarely slept and was beset by insomnia, a condition that she simply learned to incorporate into her life. But tonight, she was actually tired. Capitalizing on the unusual feeling, she got ready for bed as quickly as possible, climbed under the sheets, and turned off the light.

In her dream, there was a white rabbit insistently tapping at her front door. It wasn't until the doorbell rang that Myrtle sat up in bed. "Miles," she said.

She pulled on a robe and sleepily wandered to her front door. Myrtle peered out in the off-chance that she would see a white rabbit out there. But, as she expected, it was Miles, dressed in khakis and a button-down shirt.

Myrtle opened the door. "You didn't have to dress up, you know."

"I wasn't going to walk over here in my pajamas."

Myrtle said, "That's what I always do. In my nightgown with my robe and slippers."

"Which is likely one of the reasons Erma is convinced we're a couple," reminded Miles.

He followed Myrtle into her kitchen and sat down at the table while she made coffee and pulled out a jar of cookies.

Miles studied Myrtle as she dealt out a couple of napkins on the table. "You were asleep!" he said in great surprise.

"I do sleep occasionally, you know." Myrtle put cream and sugar on the table.

"Not at *this* time of night," said Miles.

"No, not usually. But it was a busy day. And then I had a lot of stressful nonsense with Puddin, as per usual. I capped it all off by writing a story for Sloan. I guess I was worn out." Myrtle finally sat down and they drank their coffee in silence for a minute or two.

"So, nothing from yesterday bothered you enough to keep you awake," mulled Miles.

"Yesterday? No. I regretted outliving one of my former students, but that seems to happen every day since I taught just about everyone in this town. But it certainly wasn't going to keep me *awake*." She peered at Miles over the rim of her coffee cup. "Chester's death is keeping *you* awake? You didn't even know the man aside from his billboards."

Miles sighed. "No. Nor would I have wanted to know him, from what I gather. What's bothering me is Wanda's creepy prediction."

"Her prediction? You mean her warning. It's just a warning, you know. She warns me all the time and I simply keep my head up and my eyes open and make sure to get myself *out* of danger when I finally experience it." Myrtle shrugged.

"Precisely why I'm unable to sleep. I feel the need to stay on guard." Miles shivered.

"You'll be fine, I'm sure. No one is going to break into your house and murder you in your sleep, you know. We have no idea what Wanda could be warning you about. Maybe you need to watch your step walking down stairs. Maybe you should be very careful while shaving in the mornings."

"It seemed to be food-related," said Miles. He morosely looked down at the cookies on his napkin.

"You don't really know that. Wanda simply juxtaposed a quotation from Aesop and a warning. Besides, I don't think you have to worry about store-bought cookies. Put it in perspective, Miles. The closest we've been to danger lately is in that cooking school class. I'd imagine we just need to stay sharp when we're around the likely suspects," said Myrtle.

"Staying safe would be a lot easier if I weren't enrolled in a class with them, then," said Miles.

"You can always take my attack cat home with you."

"No thank you," said Miles, glancing around him with trepidation. "Pasha's not around now, is she?"

"I think she's resting up after attacking Puddin earlier."

"Good luck getting Puddin back over here then. It'll be even harder than it usually is," said Miles.

"I know, but it was worth it. Besides, if Dusty knows he's about to get a free lawnmower, he'll be able to pressure her into coming over."

"Going back to the suspects," said Myrtle, "did you see anything? When we were outside after class, I mean. Anyone leaving the building late and looking suspicious or anyone going back inside after having been out?"

"Not a thing. I was too focused on the fact that Wanda was still there and that she had an inoperable car that I was having to address," said Miles.

Myrtle waved her hand in frustration. "I didn't see anything either. It's very annoying. I ordinarily think of myself as a very observant person."

Miles said, "It wasn't as if we thought there was anything important about our unremarkable classmates exiting a school building."

"Except one of them was remarkable. One of them was a killer. And I'm sure Red thought we were being evasive so that we could solve the case ourselves. Instead, it's just that we were being slack and not paying attention!" Myrtle thumped the table and coffee splashed up to spatter the table.

Miles looked gloomily at his napkin, now covered with coffee. "I haven't checked my email for a while. Surely we don't have class tomorrow."

"You mean *today*, remember? I'll check." Myrtle walked back into the living room to check her email. She walked back into the kitchen a minute later. "Louvenia sent a very reassuring email."

Miles relaxed in his chair. "That class is canceled for the day?"

"That 'despite the tragedy, class must go on! So much to cover! So little time!' Lots of exclamation points and drama," said Myrtle.

"That seems rather disrespectful to Chester, doesn't it?" grumbled Miles.

"It would, except for the fact that Louvenia has decreed that we'll have a 'short memorial service' at the start of class in which we'll all 'share something nice about Chester,'" said Myrtle.

Miles heaved a heavy sigh, pushing his chair backward and standing up. "On that note, I should go back home now and try to get some sleep."

"Something nice about Chester. I guess that his skill in slicing vegetables in class isn't really impressive. I suppose I'll have to choose between his skill in flying paper airplanes or shooting spitballs from when he was my student," mused Myrtle.

"Bye, Myrtle," said Miles. He walked out of the kitchen and through the living room, Myrtle trailing behind him. He opened the front door and then paused, looking down. "I suspect you'll have another visitor after me."

"What makes you say that?"

"The fact that you have a front-page story in the *Bradley Bugle*," said Miles.

"Ah! Paper's already here? Excellent. Let's hope that Sloan ran it as-is. I hate it when he tries to edit for space. And he slipped in Wanda's horoscopes, too. He's gotten a little speedier over there."

Thirty minutes after Miles left, there was indeed a knock on the door.

Myrtle knew who it was, but knowing that Red always fussed if she simply answered the door, she called out sweetly, "Who is it?"

"You know who it is," said a grumpy voice on the other side of the door.

Myrtle pulled it open. "It *could* have been Miles."

"Miles doesn't walk over here this late. He's more of a four-a.m. visitor."

"I *could* have been asleep," said Myrtle primly.

"Mama, you're awake at night more than a vampire is. And you're trying to redirect me. What I want to tell you is that you need to leave this story alone. You're close enough to it as it is, what with having been in the classroom and all. I don't need you poking your nose in where it doesn't belong. You know where that's going to lead you," said Red. He waved the newspaper at her.

"Star reporter at the local paper?" asked Myrtle.

"Dead," said Red succinctly.

"Red, it was a given that I was going to write the story. As you mentioned, I was very close to it. And it's a *big* story. Chester was an important person in this town, despite being such a terrible pupil. The story needed to be told," said Myrtle. She walked back over to her armchair and plopped down.

"I tell you what. Why don't you spend a little time with Elaine and your grandbaby today? Jack has spent a lot of time coloring lately and he can draw you a great picture," said Red.

"I've no doubt my grandson can draw an amazing picture. I've told you many times that he's a genius," said Myrtle coldly.

"Well, *that* I can't disagree with."

"Like his grandmother," said Myrtle.

Red ignored the last bit. "Anyway, Elaine has been at loose ends a little lately. And you know how difficult life is when she's bored. Sort of like *you* getting bored except no one's life gets endangered."

"What hobby is Elaine taking up now? Fencing?" asked Myrtle. "Anyway, I thought she was still refurbishing things." Her eyes settled morosely on the leering face of the gnome in her living room.

"She's backing away from the restoration a bit, and is now doing more mentoring. We're saddled with another student. Elaine volunteers at the high school with the art class. She thinks this kid, Sam, has a lot of talent." Red made a face.

"Beauty is in the eye of the beholder, Red."

"I don't think anybody's eye beholds beauty in this stuff."

Myrtle said, "What type of art is it?"

"The type I don't get."

"Well, that's a given. But there are many different *types* of art," said Myrtle.

"Some of it is performance art—I think? Some of it seems just kind of off-kilter and weird. He'll drag unusual objects onto a white surface and say it's supposed to alter our mood and thoughts about things." Red's face was baffled.

"Does it work?"

"Does what work?" asked Red.

"Does it alter your mood and thoughts?" asked Myrtle.

"It does. It makes me frustrated," said Red.

"Then it works." Myrtle shrugged. "It provokes a reaction."

"Anyway, Elaine and the teacher of the class think the kid's a genius. Although you and I will agree he's nowhere near as clever as Jack," said Red.

"No contest," replied Myrtle immediately.

"If you could check in on her? Make sure that she's not going to get inspired to follow in the kid's footsteps? The last thing I need right now is to have my house rearranged into an art exhibit." Red's eyes were pleading. "I could handle the refurbishing, but not modern art."

"Perhaps you handled the refurbishment better because there was less evidence of it in your house," said Myrtle.

She and Red stared at the gnome again. Red shivered.

Myrtle sighed. "I'll go visit her. It'll have to be sometime after my cooking class, though."

"Okay, good." Red was opening the door back up again. "By the way, I'm glad you're here."

Red's eyes were suspicious. "Why is that?"

"I need you to write me a check."

Now Red looked worried. "Everything okay, Mama? Need help paying for that cooking class or something?"

"No. I need money for a new lawnmower for Dusty. I'm surprised you could fight your way through the jungle out there. If you wait any longer, I'm going to be like Sleeping Beauty, trapped in her castle by thorny bushes," said Myrtle.

"That's extremely unlikely. It would mean that you were actually sleeping," said Red dryly. "Look, I told you I'd get him the mower and during an ordinary week I'd have already gotten it and your yard would be the best looking one in the neighborhood. But this is no ordinary week. I promise I'll get it as soon as I can."

"You could drop off the check and *I* could buy it," said Myrtle. The idea of her neighbor's yard, despite its crabgrass and other various weeds, looking better than hers was an anathema.

Red was already opening the door again. "That makes no sense, Mama. Do you know what to look for in a mower?"

"The fact that it *runs* would make it a good choice, I'd think," muttered Myrtle.

"And how would you even get it home?" Red shook his head at his mother's folly.

"Dusty could help me. Meet me at the store with his truck."

"I'd rather research the mowers and find a good one that won't cost an arm and a leg. I'd get something second-hand except it'd probably just break and we'd be stuck in the same position. Just be *patient*." With that, Red left.

Red had both warned her against investigating her story for the paper and shut down her idea for getting a mower. Myrtle decided there would be gnomes in her yard by noon so she could better express her frustration with her son. Red abhorred looking out his window across the street and seeing her collection of yard gnomes. Maybe Dusty would like to earn a little money for setting them out—especially since it didn't look as if he would be making much money mowing grass this week.

THE NEXT MORNING, MYRTLE and Miles climbed the stairs again to the classroom.

"I hope we're cooking something immensely fattening and artery-clogging today," muttered Miles as he crested the top stair.

"I'm surprised to hear you say that. You're always the one eating salads at Phil's diner. *I'm* the one eating the pimento cheese chili dogs," said Myrtle.

Miles said, "I'm in the mood for comfort food. If I can stand to eat at all, that is. My appetite might be destroyed forever by the vision of Chester lying dead in that room." He shivered.

"In that case, maybe Louvenia is planning good old-fashioned Southern funeral food. I could handle deviled eggs and ham salad with fried chicken right about now," said Myrtle.

"Didn't you just have breakfast?" the mention of fried chicken made Miles turn a little green.

"It wasn't apparently sufficient for my appetite. Toast, eggs, and bacon. It seems that I've already burned through whatever sustenance that brought me."

They walked into the classroom, which smelled strongly of disinfectant. "Amos must have had to work late yesterday," murmured Myrtle. "He wouldn't have been able to clean until the police gave him the okay."

Louvenia was decked all in black as if she were a war widow from the 1800s. The only thing missing was the diaphanous black veil. "You're the first ones here—and the last ones to have left yesterday," she said. She seemed to be enjoying her dramatic effect. "It's such a tragic, senseless death. But that's why we *needed* to have class. Food is life, and we need to celebrate life in the midst of death."

She flitted off to greet another student and Miles muttered, "Oh, brother."

"Louvenia certainly has a taste for the dramatic," agreed Myrtle. "It makes me wonder if her screaming when she found Chester was an act."

They watched as Felix came in, looking a little more subdued than he had the morning before. He still made sure to come shake Myrtle's and Miles's hands and look at them with sincerity beaming through his blue eyes. Bonnie entered and seemed a good deal more relaxed than she had yesterday. Louvenia waited another few minutes, peering into the hall from time to time.

Finally she said, "It looks as though Hattie won't be joining us today, so I guess we should just get started."

Myrtle said, "Hattie was Chester's niece. You may not have been aware of that." If Louvenia wasn't, it meant that Hattie wasn't close enough to her uncle to visit him at his office.

"*Was* she? Oh dear. Dear me. No, I didn't realize that. Oh heavens, I would never have included her in the group email if I'd known. The poor, poor child. What a terrible tragedy."

Miles sighed.

Louvenia continued on, "Well, this seems like a good time to give our special memorial for Chester before we start our class. We'll take some time to talk about him and offer some happy memories."

Bonnie had the startled look on her face of someone who hadn't done her homework. She tentatively raised her hand. "Um. Sorry, I didn't know about this." Not only did she not know about it, she seemed not to want to participate, if her white face was anything to go by.

"Oh, I sent it in my email late last night. It's nothing you really needed to *prepare* for and will only take a few minutes. I thought it would be a nice way to remember Chester and move forward after the horrible tragedy that took place here yesterday. Who would like to go first?"

Chapter Eight

Miles and Myrtle, both eager to get on with it, immediately raised their hands. Louvenia, naturally, called on Miles first.

Miles cleared his throat and looked around at the other students as he stood up. Louvenia closed her eyes as if she wanted to *feel* Miles's words. "I didn't know Chester very well. In fact, I really only knew him from his billboards around town. But he was certainly full of life. And memorable."

He sat down again quickly as his classmates clapped.

"Myrtle?" prompted Louvenia.

Myrtle stood. "It's been a long time since I had seen Chester. I found him easy to talk to yesterday—so easy to talk to that I got distracted while chopping vegetables."

Louvenia gave a trilling laugh at this, but her eyes told Myrtle that she was still considering keeping her off of tomato-chopping duty.

Myrtle continued, "I taught Chester in school many years ago. He was a very fun-loving guy." Myrtle supposed that Chester's definition of fun included making and flying paper planes and playing hangman in class instead of working on assignments. Myrtle sat down quickly to the smattering of applause.

Felix stood up without bothering to raise his hand first. His blue eyes radiated sympathy and good will. "I was proud to call Chester my friend. He was a burly guy, never much of a fancy dresser. But he had an amazing gift for business and was incredibly smart and intuitive in a non-bookish way. He had many friends."

Felix appeared to tear up and sat abruptly down. Myrtle and Miles looked at each other with eyebrows raised. Was Felix faking?

Louvenia seemed to be waiting for Bonnie to stand up and volunteer a happy memory of Chester. But Bonnie was frozen in her seat, eyes wide.

Louvenia sighed and said, "I'll go first, then. Chester Struby had a passion for life. That's evident from his desire to expand his horizons and learn how to be a better cook. Although he was only in my class for a single day, I could tell he had great promise and was going to do very well."

They applauded and Myrtle said to Miles, "No mention of her working for him at all."

Miles shrugged.

Bonnie was now in the spotlight again and seemed to be searching her brain wildly for something nice to say about the man who, from all accounts, made her life miserable in school. Finally, she stood up, quivering.

"Chester had nice suspenders," she finally stammered out before dropping with relief back into her seat.

Louvenia blinked. Then she said, "All right. Well, class, I think it's time for us to get cooking. We had a small class to begin with, which is fairly common for our continuing education classes, but now with Hattie absent and Chester gone, we'll really have to double up on our work."

"Wonderful," murmured Miles.

"We're going to start out with something easy but tasty today. A fresh take on an old favorite, tuna salad," said Louvenia.

"Then, for our next dish, we'll stretch ourselves a bit and make an entrée that will be fit to serve for all your special occasions."

The tuna salad was going fine. This time Myrtle was paired with Miles, which was actually a bit more annoying than being paired with Chester had been. For one, he took a good deal of time sanitizing their cooking station.

"I'm sure Amos did a good job," said Myrtle. "The smell of bleach could practically knock you out."

"I'd rather not put my personal safety into someone else's hands," said Miles, walking over to throw away the wipes.

Miles was putting together the tuna and fruit as Myrtle came back from the fridge with the spicy mustard. "I wonder if Hattie is planning on coming back to the class," she said.

"I hardly think so. After all, the only reason she was probably here to begin with is because her uncle was attending," said Miles.

"She certainly didn't seem to be very excited about cooking," agreed Myrtle. "Her face was the very picture of misery the times I looked over at her. Her idea of cooking is probably making a bowl of ramen. She said *al fresco* instead of *al dente*."

"Hattie wasn't *that* young. I think ramen ceases to be on the menu once one graduates from college. I bet she was here so that she could schmooze Chester somehow. Maybe to lend her some money or something," said Miles.

"Or to kill him," said Myrtle, stirring the spicy mustard vigorously into the tuna and fruit.

"That, too."

"All right, class! Let's all sample our delicious, *fancy* tuna salad," sang out Louvenia. She started handing out plates and slices of deli bread to each of them.

Miles stared into the container with misgivings. "It doesn't smell right, Myrtle."

"Of *course* it smells right."

Miles said, "It doesn't. It smells funny."

"It's tuna. It's supposed to smell funny. Besides, there are olives in there and olives always put off a different kind of smell."

Miles started peering at the various ingredients scattered on their station. "Wait a minute. What's this?"

"That? That's the spicy mustard, Miles. The *primary* ingredient in the recipe."

"This is *not* spicy mustard. Myrtle, you grabbed the wrong thing from the fridge."

Myrtle glared at him. "What are you talking about? It's a squeeze bottle of mustard."

"It's a squeeze bottle of *ginger*."

"Ginger?" Myrtle grabbed the bottle from him and held it close to her face. "What?! Why on earth would someone put ginger in a squeeze bottle? It should be in a glass jar in a pantry."

Miles rubbed his forehead as if it were beginning to throb. "Because this is *fresh* ginger. Fresh ginger must be refrigerated. This is a fancy class with fancy ingredients."

"Well, I think that's completely ridiculous. And certainly not my fault. How was I to know that they'd put ginger in a container like this? Absurd!"

Miles was now staring at the tuna salad with trepidation as if it were about to leap up out of the bowl and attack him.

Louvenia appeared suddenly in front of them, brandishing a fork. "Taste time!" she said brightly.

"Oh, I don't think so," said Miles.

Myrtle said, "I'm not particularly hungry right now. Perhaps later."

Louvenia said, "Well, *I'm* going to taste it now. I'll announce the best tuna salad in the class."

Miles and Myrtle watched silently as Louvenia took a particularly large forkful and put it in her mouth, an anticipatory smile on her lips. Her expression quickly turned to horror, her eyes grew large and she ran off for a napkin.

"I guess we win the prize. The only tuna salad in the class that wasn't actually swallowed," said Miles glumly.

Louvenia was back momentarily, looking stern. "I'm imagining that the two of you realized that there was some sort of a problem with the tuna salad?"

"Myrtle put ginger in it," offered Miles.

"It lends it a distinctive Asian flavor," said Myrtle, shooting him a look.

"Or so you would imagine, since you're not tasting it yourself," said Miles.

Fortunately, the entrée went a little better. Miles claimed the credit for that, since he stated at the start that he was going to double-check and ensure quality assurance to every ingredient going into the dish.

"We're going to have a little talk with Felix in a few minutes when class is done," said Myrtle in her stage whisper that could probably be heard from across the room.

Miles sighed. "He's a busy man. Do you think he'll stop to talk?"

"We're both voters, Miles. And the man is running for office. He'll stop and talk."

But as soon as class was over, Felix politely thanked Louvenia for teaching and fairly bolted from the classroom, pulling his phone from his pocket as he went.

"After him, Miles!" cried Myrtle.

"Wait!" called Louvenia. "Didn't you want to take home your Asian-inspired tuna salad?"

Myrtle and Miles kept hurrying along, panting.

Finally, they caught up with Felix outside. He turned at the sound of Myrtle's cane furiously hitting the pavement.

"Everything all right?" he asked pleasantly, putting his phone away.

Myrtle decided a little dithering might be in order. "As a matter of fact, Miles and I are *most shaken* by the horrible tragedy yesterday."

"Yes. Yes, we are," said Miles unconvincingly.

"Well, I can certainly understand that," said Felix in a soothing voice. "Louvenia said you were there when she discovered his body. That must have been very upsetting."

Myrtle wasn't at all sure she and Miles were really there *when* Louvenia discovered Chester's body, but she nodded anyway.

"The worst thing is, that Chester's death wasn't natural. That he was ... *murdered*." Myrtle spat out the word as though it had never crossed her lips before. Miles looked impressed at her act.

Felix nodded along as she spoke. "I agree, that's very disturbing. But the police haven't warned us to be on alert. And we have no reason to think that a killer wants to eliminate Louvenia's cooking class."

"Do you think the murderer is someone in our class?" asked Myrtle, clutching at Felix's arm as if needing strength.

To his credit, Felix tenderly covered her hand with his other one, as if comforting concerned senior citizens was a pure joy and part of his everyday life. As it might be, since he was in government in a small town.

"I suppose so. I'm expecting Red and the other authorities to be interviewing each one of us to learn what we saw or heard, or if we had a connection at all to Chester," said Felix.

"Did *you* have a connection to Chester?" asked Miles curiously.

Felix turned his friendly smile on Miles. "We were great friends, back in the day. He and I played football together, you know. Everyone knew Chester."

"Another of our cooking classmates was in your high school class, as I recall," said Myrtle.

"Bonnie," said Felix, nodding. "Poor Bonnie."

"Chester wasn't very kind to her," said Myrtle.

"Not at all. High school isn't the best time for kindness, is it? Bonnie Pendergrass unfortunately stood out a little bit. She wasn't academic, she wasn't athletic, she wasn't social. And because of that, she was something of a target. Chester could be relentless, as you know. It's how he ended up succeeding in business so well," said Felix.

"He bullied her, you mean," said Myrtle.

Felix hesitated to use a word like *bully* in reference to the dead. "I suppose you could say that."

"I certainly would. And if I'd have known about it, that would have been the end of it. The only time I saw inappropriate behavior, it involved spitballs, and I had Chester in in-school suspension." Myrtle fumed. She abhorred bullying.

Miles cleared his throat. "Myrtle and I were saying a while ago that it's frustrating that we didn't see anyone furtively leaving the building or re-entering it. We were here for a while yesterday helping a friend with car trouble. Did you see or hear anything? Notice anything unusual?"

"Where were you when Chester was murdered?" asked Myrtle more directly. Then she softened her words by forcing a smile.

Felix didn't seem to take offence. "I was actually around for a while, too. I got an important phone call and sat in my car for a while to take it. I've discovered that I'm not much of a driver when I'm talking on the phone. And I'm afraid that I was so focused on my call that I didn't notice anyone coming in or going out or doing anything at all." He gave a rueful smile.

"You didn't even notice Miles? He was working on a car in the parking lot," said Myrtle.

Felix raised his eyebrows, looking surprised.

"I wasn't *working* on the car. I was simply observing that the car no longer had any gasoline," corrected Miles.

"No, sorry, I didn't even notice you. Like I said, when I'm on a phone call, I'm laser-focused on the conversation, which is why I don't drive and talk. I wish I *had* seen something. Chester was a great guy and I'd like to make sure that his killer comes to justice. I've known Chester my entire life." Felix looked sad.

"Who do you think could have done something like this?" asked Myrtle.

"I wouldn't want to speculate," said Felix, shifting uncomfortably on his feet. "After all, I wasn't a witness and I don't even know people in the class very well."

"Of course, none of us *knows*. But who could you *imagine* doing it?"

Felix hesitated again and Miles said solemnly, "Myrtle and I aren't gossips."

"Certainly not!" said Myrtle.

Felix grinned at them. "I'd imagine not. I remember Miss Myrtle from the classroom. Smart as a whip and not one to allow for any foolishness," he said to Miles.

"Sounds about right," agreed Miles.

"This is pure speculation, but I couldn't help wondering about Bonnie," said Felix.

"Because of how hurtful Chester had been to her years ago?" asked Miles. He squinted skeptically at Felix.

"Scars last a long time. Chester annihilated her self-esteem. I ran into Bonnie at a barbeque restaurant a few years ago and we spent a few minutes catching up. She was so miserable at the time." Felix shook his head.

"She told you she was miserable?" asked Myrtle.

"She did. And the words came bubbling out of her even though I hadn't really talked with her for a couple of decades. She confided that she felt her *entire life* had been derailed during that period in high school. Before Chester had belittled and bullied her, she'd had a concrete plan of where she wanted to go to school, what she wanted to study, and what she wanted to do when she graduated."

Miles asked, "What is she doing now?"

"She's a bank teller," said Felix. "Not that there's anything wrong with that, except for the fact that *she's* not happy with it. She had hopes of being so much more than that."

"Do you think she had it in her to kill Chester?" asked Myrtle, tilting her head to one side. "I remember her as being rather timid and mousy. It's hard for me to picture."

Felix sighed. "I saw her staring at him in class yesterday. Believe me, there was hatred in her eyes. Yes, I think she could have done it. Although I have to say of all the people in the class who *might* have ended up murdered, I'm sort of surprised that it ended up being Chester."

"Who do you think would have been a more likely victim?" asked Myrtle, raising her eyebrows.

"Me," said Felix with a shrug.

Myrtle blinked at him. "You? Why on earth? You seem to be Mr. Popularity in Bradley, North Carolina. Politicians usually are."

"Well, although I was on very friendly terms with Chester, I don't think he necessarily felt the same way about me. Chester was a competitive guy—something I knew from even back when we played on the same football team. He wasn't just competitive, either ... he was furious whenever he thought I was inching my way ahead. He ended up very resentful of my success, no matter how hard he tried to conceal it." He glanced at his watch and gave them a friendly smile. "It's been nice chatting with you, but now I've got to run. See you in class tomorrow."

Chapter Nine

"So now what?" asked Miles as they got into the car.

"It seems as if there's something I'm forgetting." Myrtle pursed her lips and sat quietly in deep thought. "No. No, I can't remember it. I suppose we could forage our way through the jungle outside my house and watch our soap opera and have a snack or something."

"As long as it isn't an Asian-inspired snack." Miles's lips twisted in a smile.

"Don't be silly," said Myrtle crossly.

"What did you think about our conversation with Felix?" He followed Myrtle down her walkway and into the house.

Myrtle said, "I think there's more going on with him than he's letting on. He had such a pat answer for everything. Very smooth." She walked into the kitchen and looked in her refrigerator for inspiration.

"Naturally. He's a politician. He's very practiced at answering questions and evading inconvenient truths. He seemed to have it in for Bonnie, if you ask me. He really threw her under the bus," said Miles, taking a seat at the kitchen table.

Myrtle snapped her fingers. "That's it. What I'm trying to remember. Book club."

Miles sighed. "That's the last thing on my mind. When is it ... tomorrow? You and I haven't gone for a while. I don't even know what this month's selection was and I sure don't think I can read a book before tomorrow unless it's a very special book."

"As a matter of fact, it *is* a very special book. Special because Bonnie Pendergrass picked it out."

"What?" asked Miles. "Bonnie's not in our book club."

"Clearly you haven't been reading your emails," said Myrtle.

"I've only avoided the book club ones," said Miles.

"Bonnie is our newest member. As newest member, she got to pick the next month's selection when she joined the club."

Miles sighed. "Dare I ask what her pick for the month was?"

Myrtle peered at her cell phone to re-read the email. "It appears to be *The Heart Knows All.*"

Miles rubbed his temples as if his head hurt. "Myrtle, I don't think I could possibly read that book today. I only read books in one day if I really enjoy them."

"Now, now. You and I have become book snobs, Miles. We should open our minds to expanding our reading and opening our minds to new experiences," said Myrtle. She pulled out peanut butter, jelly, and bread and shoved them at Miles.

Miles stared glumly at the peanut butter. "Okay, clearly the real Myrtle Clover has been abducted by aliens. You're the one who said that you were avoiding book club until they started focusing on literary fiction."

"Well, maybe I want to make an exception under the circumstances. I know that our book club is full of people who wax poetic over rubbish. But if you can't beat them, join them. Here, how about we skim the book together? I'll buy it on my phone and I'll skim it really quickly and pull out the salient points."

Myrtle browsed on her phone for the book while Miles morosely spread peanut butter on a slice of bread that looked as if it had seen fresher days. "I thought the purpose of the cooking class was to improve our culinary offerings for guests," he muttered.

"Not after a mere two days of class," said Myrtle. "Don't be so unreasonable, Miles. Besides, peanut butter is a classic."

"I think you need to make a trip to the grocery store," said Miles. He peered into the jelly jar. "I'm not even sure there's enough jelly to spread over the bread."

Myrtle grinned at him. "Thanks for offering to take me."

"Wait ... what? I didn't."

"Who else will take me? Red is too busy with the case to even buy Dusty a new mower. My yard is fast becoming the Jungles of Borneo and you think he can drive me to the store?"

"Elaine drives you sometimes," said Miles, looking cranky.

"And I'm sure she would if she weren't so involved with her volunteering at the art class. She's apparently some sort of mentor to a talented kid." Myrtle paused. "Actually, that gives me an idea. Although I won't have time to act on it until after I get this book read. And maybe we can go to the store after we do our skimming. I've got a list ready to go."

"Great," said Miles flatly. "That should be around midnight. I don't see us finishing skimming a book before then."

"Oh ye of little faith. Besides, you should be happy that we're spending time reading, going to the store, and attending book club. You're the one who's so concerned about being endangered. I can't think of a safer place than my house, the grocery store, or book club." Myrtle pulled up the book, enlarged the print, and spent a few minutes in silence. "Well, it starts off with a bang. Chrissie's husband of twenty years is gone one morning, leaving the resentful Chrissie with no job and three children under the age of five. Lots of diaper changing going on."

Miles groaned.

Myrtle started skimming the book and noting plot points as she went to Miles. Fortunately, the book wasn't particularly heavy on plot. What's more, it had a reader's guide at the back of the book. Myrtle came up with some pertinent points as she went; in particular, why Chrissie would choose the insipid Randolph over the fun-loving Pierre.

"And Miles, you could start a discussion about how our approach to life choices changes as we age."

"Wonderful," said Miles morosely. "Are you sure that has something to do with the book?"

"It's *tangentially* important. And you know how book club is. They love to veer off the subject on little tangents."

Miles said, "I think of them as rabbit holes. It happens to an annoying degree."

"Anything you broach will seem reflective and astute," said Myrtle, waving a hand dismissively.

Miles looked surprised. "Why thank you, Myrtle."

"That's because those old biddies think that everything that comes out of your mouth is golden. You know what a hot commodity you are in Bradley. What with driving and everything."

Miles's lips tightened together in a thin line.

Once Myrtle and Miles returned from the grocery store, Miles helped her unload her groceries and then quickly left before Myrtle found something else for him to do.

"See you tomorrow for class!" said Myrtle.

Miles looked as if the thought of class gave him indigestion.

Myrtle picked up the phone. She'd told Red that she'd check in on Elaine anyway. And now she had a great idea. "Elaine? Hi there. How are you and how is my darling grandchild?"

Elaine laughed. "A little less darling than usual today, but cute as always. How are things going?"

"Oh, you know—always busy around here. Actually, I had a question for you. The last time I saw Red, he mentioned that you were mentoring an art student," said Myrtle.

Elaine said, "I am! Myrtle, Sam Sinclair is wonderful. Really gifted. But he has had a very tough upbringing and I don't think his family understands art or him, and they don't encourage him at all. The high school class has a participation fee because of all the supplies that they need, but he couldn't afford to pay it. Sam washed Red's and my car and did a few odd chores for the money. Did you need him to mow your lawn for you?"

Myrtle sighed. "It sounds like heaven, but Dusty's lawnmower is broken. You must not have been able to catch up with Red much to hear about the saga. I'd hire another yard man to come out, but I'd feel as if I were letting Dusty down. And letting Red off the hook! At least this way my yard serves as a di-rectly-across-the-street reminder for Red. Which brings me to the point of my call."

"You need his number? There's some other chore he can do for you?" asked Elaine.

"Indeed. There is some other chore," said Myrtle.

Cooking class the next day was a bit of a non-event, as far as Myrtle was concerned. She and Miles had arrived slightly late for class and Louvenia hadn't particularly wanted to repeat what they'd missed. She'd learned all about cooking techniques and shortcuts, but she and Miles were able to ferret out *no* information from any of the fellow students. Louvenia had been a bit of a nuisance and paired Myrtle and Miles together again so that Myrtle had no chance to ask anyone else questions. Hattie was absent once again, although Louvenia said that Hattie had sworn to 'bravely make it' to the next class. Bonnie was rather withdrawn. The only time she brightened was when Myrtle found a couple of seconds to tell her that she was looking forward to discussing her selection at book club later that afternoon.

On the upside, Louvenia had finally done her 'special event' class and Myrtle now had a menu for her dinner party. After finishing the dish, which Miles had annoyingly mostly prepared, Myrtle cleared her throat and said, "By the way, I wanted to let everyone know that I'll be hosting a dinner party and coffee at a date to be announced!"

Everyone blinked at her and Louvenia's eyes were cloudy with concern.

Myrtle frowned. "Nothing to be concerned about. It's merely a way to practice what I've learned."

"It sounds delightful," said Louvenia in a falsely cheerful voice. "Do keep us appraised as to the time and date of the event." She hurriedly moved on to cover what the next class would be covering.

Miles was gloomy as they walked out of the building after class. "I'm in danger and you're inviting a bunch of murder suspects to a dinner party I'm attending?"

"You know it'll be a great way to investigate. I can really add some pizazz to my next article for Sloan. It'll be more of a 'special report' on progress in the case. But never mind that. Are you ready for book club?"

"Am I *ever* ready for book club?" asked Miles as he drove away.

"You remember the point that you're making for the discussion?"

"Of course. I pretend that this is a worthwhile book with worthwhile areas to discuss. I mention that the choices we make as we age may change." Miles shrugged.

"I'm hoping we can catch Bonnie at the beginning or end of the meeting and really get a chance to talk to her," said Myrtle. "She's simply not easy to catch up with at cooking class."

"I get the impression she's not trying to make friends," said Miles. "Or maybe she doesn't like us."

Myrtle glared at him. "Of *course* she likes us, Miles. Everyone does. She's merely shaken by what happened in that classroom. The fact that someone was murdered makes her jumpy. She seems nervous and she scrambles away during breaks and at the end of the class. It's very frustrating. With any luck, she'll be more relaxed at book club."

The rest of the drive was consumed by talk of their soap opera and what the characters were up to. Miles slowed the car down as he approached Myrtle's driveway. "Who is that?"

"Oh! I completely forgot. What time is it? Okay, well, at least I'm not late," said Myrtle.

Miles said, "So you know who this is?"

There was a young man standing in Myrtle's jungle of a front yard. He was dressed in a black shirt and black pants and probably had black shoes on, although they couldn't see because of the height of the grass. He had several earrings in a variety of places and some visible tattoos.

"Naturally. This is Sam. He's an artist that Elaine is mentoring. I have a project for him."

"I can't wait to find out what that is," murmured Miles. "Okay, I'll see you in a couple of hours for book club, then."

He drove away as Myrtle reached out her hand in greeting to the young artist. "Sam? Good to meet you."

He shook her hand and said a little shyly, "Good to meet you too, Mrs. Clover."

"As you know, I've asked you here because I wanted to commission a work. You got the photo I emailed you?"

Sam nodded.

"Good. And you brought some props and other things to work with?" asked Myrtle.

"They're in my car," said Sam, gesturing to a small, very old sedan nearby.

"That's great. But before I commission this project, I need you to understand something about it—it won't last long. It's the kind of artwork that will be created for brief, maximum impact and then will likely be removed." She peered at the young man with concern.

But Sam was nodding his head calmly. "Impermanence. I've been learning in school that there are many artists experimenting with impermanent art."

"Really?" Myrtle blinked.

"It's supposed to be a part of life and can represent its painful transitions. Besides, I'll take lots of pictures of it when it's done." He grinned at Myrtle.

"Perfect! All right, here's what I want you to do."

Myrtle went in to eat and watch *Tomorrow's Promise* before book club. She could hear Sam working outside from time to time and smiled to herself. Occasionally, he knocked on the door and asked her if she had particular items. She would hand them to him and then go back to watching her show.

She realized she had evidence of cooking school smattered on her blouse and changed a few minutes before Miles was due to pick her up. When she walked back out to her living room and heard voices outside, she smiled again and peered out the window.

Her neighbor, Erma Sherman's, strident voice was raised and she was gesturing wildly with her hands. Miles, staring out his car window, looked at her yard in wonderment.

Chapter Ten

Sam the Artist looked calm as he put the finishing touches on his gnome-inspired masterpiece. He'd pulled just enough gnomes out of Myrtle's shed to make little vignettes in the yard. One gnome held up a sign that said, "Help me. I'm lost in a jungle." One appeared to be doing battle with the grass with a child-sized rake and hoe that Myrtle kept in her shed for Jack to play with. One lay on the ground, apparently overcome by Myrtle's yard. Sam had figured out a way for Myrtle's warrior gnome to be brandishing a weed trimmer at her surprised-looking gnome. Funny, poignant little vignettes of chaos that should jog Red's memory about Dusty's broken mower.

As soon as loud Erma had waddled away, Myrtle hurried outside with a handful of money. "Sam, it's perfect. You're a genius. It's exactly what I'd envisioned."

Miles just continued staring blankly at the scene from the car.

Sam beamed at Myrtle. "Thanks! I kind of hate to stop working on it. It was a lot more fun than I thought it would be. Maybe, if I have some more ideas, I can come by later to work on it."

Miles was now getting out of the car and walking cautiously toward them as if the gnomes might suddenly explode from Myrtle's yard and come at him with their yard equipment. "This is ... different, Myrtle."

"It's yard art," said Myrtle grandly. "What exactly would you call it, Sam? You're the art prodigy."

Sam absently wiped some dirt from his hands onto his black jeans. "I'm calling it post-modern: the art of yard art."

"Brilliant," said Myrtle. She handed the money to Sam. "Thanks so much. If you need a reference, let me know." She tilted her head to one side. "Do artists *need* references?"

"Maybe a blurb for my website?" asked Sam.

Miles seemed impressed that Sam had a website.

Several minutes later, Miles was driving Myrtle to Tippy Chambers' house. "Red is going to flip out, you know."

"What else is new?" asked Myrtle with a shrug. "I'd think that he'd be relieved that I was exploring my artistic side. Or, rather, outsourcing that exploration to Sam. What a talented kid!"

"He might look at it as evidence that you need to be yard-free. I'm thinking he's going to be making more inquiries at Greener Pastures retirement home regarding your possible admission."

"It's not like it would be the first time he's done that. Besides, if he's too busy to get Dusty a new lawnmower, he's too busy to get me committed to a retirement home," said Myrtle.

"*Committed* is a strong word. It's not an asylum," said Miles.

"Isn't it?"

They pulled in front of Tippy's large, columned house, next to one of the massive magnolia trees that shielded the house from the road.

They were about to knock on the door when it was suddenly pulled open. Tippy, chic as usual, was wearing a silky red blouse paired with immaculate white slacks. "Hello, you two!" she said, giving them both a hug. "I was getting worried that you'd both decided to quit book club. It's been too long since we've seen you."

Myrtle bared her teeth in a smile. "We've missed book club. Haven't we, Miles?"

Miles nodded unhappily.

"Well, you've both made my day that you're here."

They walked into a large living room filled with portraits of stiffly-sitting, scowling ancestors and brightly-polished silver.

"Oh *no*," said Myrtle. "Erma is here. I thought she wasn't ever really attending book club anymore."

"Another excellent reason to stop going ourselves," murmured Miles.

At least Erma was deep in conversation with Georgia Simpson, who was bellowing with laughter at Erma. Georgia was probably the only person in town who could effectively handle Erma's obnoxious behavior. Georgia had very big hair that was sprayed into submission, mascara-encrusted eyes, and sported tattoos over her arms and legs. Myrtle had recently seen Georgia smoking cigars on a sidewalk in downtown Bradley. Miles had always been rather fascinated with her, and now he proceeded to gape.

Myrtle steered him toward the refreshments table. "Food and beverages ... and Bonnie ... over here, Miles."

Bonnie was looking as hapless as ever but greeted them with a shy smile. "I guess we're spending a lot of time together, aren't we? Considering we're in book club together and all. Y'all weren't at the last meeting, I don't think. That's when I joined."

"Or the meeting before that, or the meeting before that," intoned Miles.

"But we're delighted to be here with you today," said Myrtle, cutting Miles off smoothly before he revealed that it had been the book club Christmas party where they had last made an appearance. "And we of course read your pick for the meeting," she added politely.

Bonnie gasped. "Wasn't it wonderful? I cried and cried."

Miles raised his eyebrows at Myrtle. Myrtle and he somehow hadn't gotten the message that the book was particularly emotional one way or another during their skim session.

"Yes. A very heartfelt book," said Myrtle. "But I won't go into the book any more, since the club likes us to save our discussion for the meeting. So we'll move on to something else. Are you enjoying the cooking class?"

A shadow fell across Bonnie's eyes. "I suppose so. I mean, Louvenia is a doing a good job teaching and she's very enthusiastic about the food."

"She certainly is." Myrtle could stand for a little less of the bubbly-Louvenia and a little more of a serious instructor.

"But, the ... well ... the death. It was ...." Bonnie shivered.

Myrtle and Miles leaned in to listen, but jumped back when a shrill voice said, "Well, looky-here! Myrtle and Miles, two peas in a pod!"

Bonnie looked like a deer in the headlights, mumbled an excuse, and left Myrtle and Miles with Myrtle's nemesis and neighbor, Erma. Erma was grinning at them, her large front teeth sticking out prominently.

"Glad to see you here, Myrtle. I was going to ask you what on earth was happening in your yard?" demanded Erma.

Myrtle maneuvered herself back a little from Erma's horrid breath and said coldly, "It's yard art, Erma. Post-modern. Art about art."

Georgia strutted over to join them. "Hi there! Hey, I wanted to know about your yard, too. What is it again?"

"It's a post-modern art exhibit. It's meant to be tongue-in-cheek. A brilliant young man created it," said Myrtle.

"Hmm." Georgia considered this. "Interesting. Of course, I wouldn't want to have anything happen to my angel collection, although I do like the idea of doing something different with them. You know, give them a job to do and make them feel better about themselves."

Miles gave Myrtle a look. Georgia had very unusual artistic sensibilities.

Erma leaned in to make a point and everyone else leaned back out. "What I don't get is the tall grass and weeds. What's that all about? What has that got to do with the art?"

Myrtle said, "It's the whole backdrop. The gnomes are fighting for their lives against the jungle of the yard. It's an analogy for life, isn't it?"

Georgia looked startled. "Well, whutdoya know? You're right. It's an analogy thing."

"No talking about book club until the discussion starts, ladies!" reminded Tippy with a gracious smile.

Erma spat out a laugh. "We're not talking about books. We're talking about Myrtle's yard."

Tippy was clearly trying to remain her usual polite hostess self although the curiosity was apparently eating her up inside. "Myrtle's yard ... yes, I think I saw a very interesting ... display. Out of the corner of my eye. Is that ... well, what exactly is it?"

"It's art," said Myrtle shortly. "The kind of art you have to think about."

"I do like art, but I don't always get it," said Erma. "And the last time I went to see a traveling art exhibit in Charlotte, I got so sick there! It was food poisoning—I went to one of those fancy sushi restaurants, you see."

Tippy, very subtly, moved away to join another group of members.

"I didn't feel sick at *first*, you know. But then, as I was at the museum, I started feeling really, really *awful*," said Erma.

Miles looked sadly at Myrtle. They avoided Erma as much as they possibly could, but sometimes they couldn't get rid of her. And now they were stuck with her instead of spending time with Bonnie, which was the whole reason they were at book club to begin with.

As they stared at Erma, resigned to their doom, suddenly Georgia bellowed in interruption, "Have you met our visitor today? A cousin of Tippy's who's visiting from Germany."

Miles and Myrtle beamed in great relief at a slender woman in glasses with a kind smile. "I'm Nicole Teschke. Tippy invited me to book club and I'm so excited to be here—I love books and reading."

"A serious reader?" asked Myrtle in pity. She lowered her voice, "Then I'll apologize in advance since this isn't a very serious book club."

Erma, always wanting to focus the conversation back on herself and her legion of medical issues, quickly said, "You know, Nicole, *I've* been to Germany before. It was a long time ago, when I was a student. The only thing was that I became terribly sick while I was there—"

On that note, Myrtle grabbed Miles by the arm and hurried him away.

Miles looked back at Nicole, politely listening to Erma go on and on. "I feel sorry about dumping that nice young lady with Erma. She saved us from a terrible fate."

"Me too, but not bad enough to suffer another moment with Erma," said Myrtle with a shudder. "Isn't this blasted meeting supposed to be starting up?"

"Ladies? It's time to start our meeting," called Tippy.

"Saved by the bell," muttered Miles.

"Bonnie? Would you like to come up and talk a little about the book? Maybe what drew you to it? And then we'll have a round-robin discussion about it," said Tippy briskly.

Bonnie turned bright red and reluctantly stood and walked to the front of the living room. She said in a low voice, "I chose *The Heart Knows All* because I wanted to read something really positive and optimistic, and I thought that's what the book would be."

Erma snorted loudly from the back of the room and said to Nicole, "As if!"

Bonnie continued talking, or rather, mumbling, about the book while Miles leaned over and whispered to Myrtle, "Wasn't the book very chipper and optimistic? I thought that's what we'd gathered from it."

"Of course it is! Erma doesn't know anything about books. She probably didn't read the thing," hissed Myrtle back.

"I don't think we can really talk," said Miles stiffly.

"That was lovely," said Tippy. "Thank you, Bonnie."

Bonnie hurried back to her seat in great relief.

Tippy smiled graciously at them, the perfect hostess as usual. "Welcome to everyone, including our guest, my cousin Nicole, and our newest member, Bonnie, who presented us with this month's selection. One reason I'm so delighted to be here this month is because our own Myrtle Clover is here."

"Finally graced us with her presence," cackled Erma from the back.

Tippy ignored the interruption. "As most of you know, Myrtle is a retired English teacher. Actually, many of us had the pleasure of having Myrtle as a teacher."

Myrtle sighed, looking around at the middle-aged and elderly faces that were beaming at her. It was true, but did it have to be pointed out? The ladies gave her a round of applause. She gritted her teeth and managed to grimace a grin.

"I always look forward to Myrtle's insightful analysis of each selection. Let's hear from Myrtle first and then proceed around the room clockwise," said Tippy.

Miles made a muffled sound that very likely was suppressed hysteria. Myrtle dug her elbow into his side.

Myrtle decided that the best way to proceed was to do so in complete confidence. If she could present her analysis in a self-assured manner, she was sure to sound as if she'd done more than skim the pages of *The Heart Knows All*.

"Although I didn't originally suspect that the book would be heavy in literary devices or theme, I was pleasantly surprised to find an abundance of them in the novel. Especially the author's use of dramatic irony." Myrtle glanced around, hopeful that the now well-fed ladies would be nodding off to sleep and not listening to her, but to her chagrin, they appeared to be keenly interested.

Myrtle sighed and continued, "As readers, we knew Clarissa was betraying Chrissie with Randolph. Which made Chrissie's interactions with Clarissa late in the story especially poignant."

Bonnie's face was bewildered. "I don't understand, Miss Myrtle."

"Don't understand dramatic irony? Well, it's been a very long time since you were in my class, Bonnie. I could refresh everyone's memory, if you'd like." Myrtle was eager to talk about something she really *did* know about and remove herself from the morass of the book as soon as possible.

Tippy said with her careful enunciation, "I believe, Myrtle, that Bonnie doesn't understand how Clarissa would have interacted with Chrissie late in the story."

Myrtle frowned. "The usual way. Talked to her. Or the modern equivalent: texted or emailed or something."

"But Clarissa drowned in chapter four," said Tippy gently, now searching Myrtle's face for signs of a possible medical event.

Miles made a strangled noise and hid his face in his hands, shoulders shaking silently.

The ladies looked alarmed and Myrtle patted Miles's knee. "Clarissa's untimely demise always makes Miles tearful. He's so sensitive, you know. Perhaps we'd be wise to avoid mentioning her for the time being."

Tippy's eyes were now a bit suspicious. She wouldn't dare ask Myrtle outright if she'd read the book, though.

"It was a lovely book," said Myrtle, smiling encouragingly at Bonnie. "I only wish the author had taken care not to name two characters with such similar names. Clarissa and Chrissie. What on earth was that writer thinking?"

There was some more scattered applause from the back of the room from other confused readers. Myrtle smiled in satisfaction. She'd at least made a very salient point.

"Your thoughts, Miles?" asked Tippy, looking at Miles in concern. Miles's hands covered his mouth now, a marked improvement from covering his entire face.

Miles lowered his hands and said, "It was an interesting book. It made me think about how the ... um ... choices that we make in life change as we get older." He looked around hopefully at the other book club members. But everyone seemed confused.

Tippy said, "But the main characters in the story were all millennials, Miles. They were all in their twenties."

Miles said, stumbling over his words in his rush, "That's exactly what I mean. Why would Chrissie choose Randolph over the fun-loving Pierre?"

Myrtle could see that the book club members desperately wanted to agree with Miles. Most of them harbored secret fantasies of standing at the altar with Miles Bradford beside them. But they just couldn't quite figure out where he was coming from.

Tippy said sharply, "But Chrissie *didn't* choose Randolph. Randolph was grief-stricken over the tragic death of Clarissa and ended up drinking himself to death."

This statement prompted another muffled outburst from Miles, which he quickly covered up, hurriedly excusing himself as he strode in the direction of Tippy's downstairs powder room.

Myrtle clicked her tongue. "He's just devastated over that Clarissa."

The ladies looked wistfully after him.

Chapter Eleven

Finally, blessedly, the meeting drew to a close. As the ladies all rushed over to comfort poor Miles over his devastation at Clarissa's death, Myrtle rushed over oriental rugs and past stately antique furniture to find Bonnie and force her into having a few words with her before she left. She *wouldn't* allow Bonnie to go flying out of there as she did at cooking class. But where had the woman gone?

Myrtle finally entered the kitchen, startling Tippy's housekeeper, who leapt to her feet to stand stiffly at attention. Myrtle briefly thought that she was going to salute her.

"Have you seen a woman about so high? With thick glasses?" asked Myrtle quickly.

The housekeeper nodded. "She took a bunch of food and headed that way." She bobbed her head in the direction of the front door.

Myrtle rushed out of the kitchen and toward the door, cane thumping furiously on the parquet floor as she went.

As she hurried out onto Tippy's verandah, she saw Bonnie carrying a large amount of party food, heading with great purpose toward a dilapidated vehicle.

"Bonnie!" called Myrtle desperately. She didn't want to hurry down Tippy's steep, deep front steps. The last thing she needed right now was for Red to start really focusing on her as the result of taking a spill down Tippy's stairs.

Bonnie jumped and swung around, eyes startled. She looked down with anxious eyes at her armfuls of food and said, "It all looked so good that I thought I'd have a little snack later."

Myrtle thought it looked as if it might be enough food to sustain Bonnie for several days. She said kindly, "Is everything all right, Bonnie?"

Bonnie's eyes filled with tears behind the thick lenses of her glasses. "No, no it's really not. The reason I'm able to do book club is because I lost my job."

"What? But you've been a teller at the bank for ages. I won't know what to do if I don't see you at the bank anymore," said Myrtle.

Bonnie's eyes grew even more teary and one slipped out, trickling its way down her cheek. Myrtle shifted on her feet. Crying was something she'd rather not deal with and was ill-equipped to handle. She rifled through her purse for a tissue and briskly handed it to Bonnie, who swabbed her face with one hand while still clutching a couple of tea sandwiches in the other hand.

"They're cutting back on staff. Say they don't need as many of us," said Bonnie, her lip trembling.

"But what about the cooking class? I thought that anyone signed up for a cooking class must be rather affluent," said Myrtle. "Or at least not destitute."

Bonnie said, "Oh, my mother paid for the class. She knew I'd always loved cooking and she thought that maybe I could learn enough to be able to work for a restaurant or something."

Behind them were the sounds of a couple of book club members coming out Tippy's front door. Bonnie turned bright red. "I've got to go," she muttered and hurried off.

"Pooh!" said Myrtle in disgust. Usually the book club spent at least a half-hour visiting after each meeting. And now her suspect had been chased away.

She was looking after Bonnie sadly when Tippy's cousin, Nicole, walked up to her. Myrtle smiled at her. "You don't know it, but you saved me today."

Nicole raised her eyebrows and said in her charmingly accented English, "I assume you mean from the lady I was speaking with."

"Yes, except Erma Sherman is no lady," said Myrtle with a shudder. "And, sadly, she's my next-door neighbor. I spend way too much time and energy trying to escape her or making sure the coast is clear before I walk out of my house."

Nicole said, "I can see why. Although she did tell me a couple of interesting things."

Myrtle laughed. "Are you sure we're talking about the same person? The only thing Erma ever knows how to talk about is her horrifying and countless health problems."

"She did plenty of that. But she also told me that you were a sleuth." Nicole gave Myrtle an interested look.

Myrtle preened. "She's right about that, actually. I just try to help my son out when I can. He's the police chief here."

"I saw you trying to catch up with ... Bonnie, wasn't it? Does she have something to do with the murder Tippy was telling me about?"

"Maybe, maybe not. I was hoping that she at least had some sort of information she could give me, but who knows? She ran off like a rabbit and I didn't get a thing from her." Myrtle watched in frustration as Bonnie's old car sputtered out of the driveway and puttered into the street.

"That's one reason why I thought Erma was interesting. She told me something about Bonnie," said Nicole.

Myrtle turned her full attention on the young woman. "Is that so? I would be very grateful if you'd share it with me. You'd have spared me once again from having to talk to Erma and ask her about it."

"She said that she and Bonnie were the first ones here. I was busy helping Tippy get food and drinks and chairs set out. Erma said that while she was talking to Bonnie, Bonnie was very flustered and said she was nervous about speaking to the book club. She was juggling her book, her purse, and her car keys and dropped her purse. A letter fell out, according to Erma. Apparently, it was a very angry letter to a man named Chester," said Nicole.

Myrtle raised her eyebrows. "Now *that* is interesting."

"Chester is the man who was killed, isn't he?" asked Nicole.

"He is indeed," said Myrtle.

"She had proximity to him, too?" asked Nicole.

"She did. Of course, technically, *I* did, too. But I had nothing against Chester except that he was a disruption in my classroom decades ago," said Myrtle.

Nicole said, "I'm surprised that Erma would tell me about what she saw. She didn't even know me."

"Not knowing someone wouldn't stop Erma. I'm not at all surprised that she told you about it," said Myrtle. "Erma is the type of person who likes to *know* things. And she's also the kind of person who likes to gossip."

"It's a wonder that *she* hasn't gotten murdered then," said Nicole thoughtfully.

"Isn't that the truth?" said Myrtle. "Well, you've been incredibly helpful and I really appreciate it. Did you enjoy book club?" she asked politely.

"I did, although the book might not have been my pick. But I love books—to read and just to surround myself with. I even made a Christmas tree out of a book last year," said Nicole.

"Amazing. You should talk to my daughter-in-law, Elaine. She's always trying to be crafty. Unfortunately, her attempts are rarely successful," said Myrtle. "Although I admire her persistence." Miles walked up to join them and Myrtle said, "Good to meet you, Nicole."

Miles murmured as they walked toward his car, "Finally. I'm ready to make our getaway."

Myrtle said caustically, "Are you sure? Usually you enjoy being the only rooster in the hen house."

They turned as Tippy rushed outside, "Is Bonnie still here?"

"I'm afraid not," said Myrtle, still irked by her sudden departure.

Tippy sighed. "She forgot her purse."

Myrtle said, "We'll get it to her."

"Really?" asked Tippy, although her expression was relieved. "Myrtle, won't that be something of a pain?"

Miles said under his breath, "Yes, won't that be something of a pain?"

"Not a bit. I'm happy to see it safely home," said Myrtle with alacrity.

Myrtle and Miles climbed into his car. "I was sort of hoping this farcical day could come to a close," said Miles as he started up the car.

"You mean that you didn't enjoy our lovely book club meeting?" asked Myrtle. "You certainly seemed to be enjoying it. I've never heard so much suppressed laughter in my life."

Miles said, "They were just so earnest about the book. And we were making up discussion questions. I believe it drove me to hysteria."

Miles glanced over at Myrtle and frowned. "Hey, what ... what are you doing, Myrtle?"

"I'm searching Bonnie's purse," said Myrtle calmly, peering inside the big, battered, bag.

"You shouldn't do that," said Miles, eyebrows puckered.

"Why not? We need to find out exactly where Bonnie lives in order to get her purse back, don't we? And it's not as if I *stole* the bag. We're doing her a tremendous favor, returning it to her," said Myrtle, pulling out a sheet of stationery with roses printed on it.

Miles said dryly, "Yes, I can see that you're focusing on her driver's license to get the address."

Myrtle frowned as she studied the piece of paper. "It's just like Erma said."

"You spoke to *Erma* today? Was that telepathically? I don't recall seeing the two of you even on the same side of the room as each other." Miles pulled the car to the side of the road.

"No, I didn't speak to her. But the guest, Nicole, did. Erma told her that Bonnie had written a very angry letter to Chester. Bonnie dropped it and Erma read it and blabbed to Nicole about it," said Myrtle. She glanced around the car and said, "Okay, right, the driver's license for the address. Let's see. It's 123B. Mill Street."

Miles resumed driving again. "What does the letter say?"

"Basically, it calls Chester a lot of names and says that he ruined her life," said Myrtle.

Miles said, "What I don't understand is why she'd write him a letter to begin with, if she was going to kill him."

"Who knows? Maybe she planned on just handing him the letter, but when she saw him, her rage made her kill him. We can ask her—this is 123B right here," said Myrtle.

The duplex was small and looked as if it had seen better days. The yard was sketchily covered with a weedy grass.

"This is it?" asked Miles, somewhat doubtfully.

"Chester ruined her life, remember?" said Myrtle as she got out of the car.

Myrtle had to knock on the door twice before it was somewhat guardedly pulled open on a chain. Bonnie peered suspiciously out.

"Bonnie? It's Myrtle and Miles. We've come to return your purse," said Myrtle.

Bonnie, who had food in her mouth that she was rapidly trying to swallow, knitted her brows in confusion. She put a hand over her mouth and said, "Purse?"

"You left it. At book club," said Miles in the kind of patient voice you would use with a rather dense preschooler.

"Oh!" Bonnie closed the door, removed the chain, and hurriedly opened the door. Her face was blotched with red in her embarrassment. "Here, let me take it off your hands. I'm so sorry."

Myrtle wasn't about to let this go at the door, not after being thwarted when Bonnie escaped Tippy's house. "May we come in? Miles mentioned that he needed to use the facilities." She leaned in and said in a whisper to Bonnie, "You know how frequently older men need a restroom."

Miles shot her a furious look but said stiffly, "Yes. If it isn't too much trouble, Bonnie."

"Of course not. And thanks so much for taking the trouble of coming all the way out here to return my purse. I've been so scatterbrained lately." Bonnie stepped aside and ushered them into a small living room. Miles obediently disappeared into the back of the house.

Myrtle doubted that Bonnie had been scatterbrained only *lately*. She rather thought it had been a lifelong affliction. "You won't mind if I sit down." It wasn't a question. There were some benefits of age and sitting wherever and whenever you wanted to was one of them.

"Of course not," repeated Bonnie in a miserable voice. She gathered papers and other clutter, shoving them into a nearby coat closet to make room for Myrtle and Miles to sit.

It looked as if Bonnie had also spent the few minutes she'd been home busily stress-eating. There were crumbs on her top and there was evidence on the coffee table of the crust-less pimento cheese sandwiches that Tippy had prepared.

Myrtle decided that Bonnie was so elusive that she had to go to the next step in dealing with her. She needed to revert to being Bonnie's schoolteacher again.

"Now Bonnie," she said in a scolding voice, "I've been trying to have a conversation with you and I can't imagine that you've been unaware of this. And yet you've bolted from the cooking class and bolted from book club." She paused for effect. "It makes you seem as if you might have something to hide."

"What? No." Bonnie's face was full of panic.

"I'm afraid it does. I should also tell you that while I was searching for your driver's license to find your address, I found a curious letter in your purse." Myrtle gave Bonnie a stern look. "Would you like to explain it?"

Bonnie looked as if she definitely would *not* like to explain it. She stammered, "I think the letter says it all."

"Well, it certainly says a lot. It says that you felt traumatized and stunted by Chester's appalling behavior in school. It fairly simmers with resentment and rage. But one of the things I thought was interesting was that it was written in the present tense. Was it written before Chester's death?" asked Myrtle.

Bonnie's shoulders sank. "It was. Barely. I was shocked to find out that the one person in this town that I *didn't* want to spend time with was in a cooking class with me. That I might have to be *partners* with him!"

"You couldn't just make up an excuse for Louvenia and drop out of the class?" asked Myrtle.

Miles joined them, sitting gingerly down next to Myrtle.

"I'd feel bad doing that. Like I told you, my mother signed me up for the course and spent money she really didn't have because she thought I might find it useful. I'd feel bad not getting anything out of it. And Mother never really knew about Chester

Struby because I was too ashamed to tell her how awful he was in school," said Bonnie.

Myrtle's eyes narrowed. "I really, really wish that you had told *me*, Bonnie. I'd have straightened him out for you."

Bonnie gave her a shy smile. "You actually helped without even knowing about it. One time you saw something. I don't think you even knew what you'd seen, but you realized Chester was belittling me or something. The next thing I knew, Chester was getting in-school suspension for a week." She sighed happily. "That was a wonderful week."

Myrtle nodded. "I only wish I'd known the extent to which the bullying was happening. On to the letter, though. When did you write it?"

"During class. I was supposed to be learning cooking terms, I guess. I decided it would be healthy to express my feelings on paper instead of letting them boil up inside me," said Bonnie.

Miles said, "Were you planning on giving it to him?"

"I wasn't sure if I could work up the courage to do that. But at least I did feel better after I'd written it. I stuffed it into my purse," said Bonnie.

"And you carry rose-covered stationery around with you?" asked Myrtle, raising her eyebrows.

"It reminds me to write notes to my mother," said Bonnie. "She lives in a retirement home a couple of hours away and I don't get to visit her as often as I'd like. Sometimes I have a little extra time in a doctor's waiting room or waiting to get my oil changed and I'll jot a few lines to her. She doesn't do computers."

"So what happened after class?" asked Myrtle.

Bonnie looked steadily down at the floor and took a deep breath. "First of all, I never wanted him to *die*. I think I feel worse now than I did before. I feel like all my negative thoughts and bad wishes contributed to his death."

Miles said, "Negative thoughts and bad wishes don't kill people."

Bonnie gave him a grateful look. "That's true. But it's how I've been feeling. After class, I ... as you said ... bolted. I didn't want to give him the chance to say something mean. I feel like I've come a long way since high school. You know—I didn't let Chester *define* me as a victim."

Myrtle and Miles shared a glance. Myrtle said slowly, "But Felix mentioned that he'd seen you recently and that you felt your life had been 'derailed' by Chester."

Chapter Twelve

Bonnie flushed. "Maybe some days I feel that way. But not always. Anyway, after class I hurried out of there. I've been trying to lose a little weight and once I got out of the building and into the fresh air, the campus was so pretty that I decided to take a little walk."

Miles cleared his throat. "That's funny. We didn't see you."

"Pardon me?" asked Bonnie, looking alarmed.

"Myrtle and I didn't see you taking your walk. She and I were at the school for a long time because a friend of ours had car trouble," said Miles.

"And then there was a murder discovered," added Myrtle.

Bonnie shifted from one foot to another. "I don't know why I didn't see you. Maybe it's just that I took a walk in a different direction."

"When were you planning on giving him the note?" asked Myrtle.

Bonnie said, "I wasn't even sure I *could* give it to him or if I *should* give it to him. I wondered if maybe that would start things up again. I didn't want to start any trouble with him, even all these years later."

Miles said, "It most likely was someone in our cooking class that killed Chester, you know."

Bonnie grew even more solemn. "I gathered that. Red came to speak to me." She turned to Myrtle. "He was very kind to me."

"He'd better be," said Myrtle. "That's how I raised him. So he's been around trying to get more information. Did you give him any? Did you have any ideas who might have murdered Chester?"

Bonnie said quickly, "Well, I don't have any proof, of course. Not having been there. But if I had to pick someone, I'd think his niece might have something to do with it."

"Hattie? What makes you think so?" asked Myrtle.

"A few things. For one, she's living beyond her means," said Bonnie.

"She is?" Myrtle considered this. The only real impression she'd gotten of Hattie so far was that she was bored in cooking class and that she had a fondness for wearing black.

Bonnie nodded. She paused and then said in a hurry, "I was her bank teller. I don't want to disclose any information I'm not supposed to, but I can say that Hattie has a fondness for making big purchases and eating out. With her income, there's no way she could keep that up for very long."

Miles said, "Was she overdrawn a lot?"

Bonnie nodded vigorously.

"You're saying that she murdered her uncle for his money?" asked Myrtle.

"It sounds terrible to say, but I think it must be true. I know that Hattie is Chester's only living relative. Hattie's father, Chester's brother, died in a car accident in Atlanta some time ago. And his parents have been dead for ages," said Bonnie.

Apparently, even though Bonnie was terrified of Chester, she still kept up with what was going on in his life through the *Bradley Bugle*.

"When you were taking your walk, though, you didn't *see* anything? You didn't see Hattie go back into the building?" asked Myrtle.

"No, I didn't see a thing." She gave an unhappy laugh. "Maybe that's what that horoscope in the paper meant: *open your eyes*. Anyway, I thought the walk would calm my nerves a little and help me stay on track to lose weight, too. But instead, I ended up replaying in my head the moment when I saw him in the classroom. I ended up so keyed up that I walked right back to my car and drove straight home," said Bonnie.

Bonnie clearly didn't have anything else to contribute and was stealing glances at the party food again, so Myrtle and Miles said their goodbyes.

"Oh, and Bonnie?" asked Myrtle before she walked out the door. "I'm having a dinner party and coffee to practice all the skills we've learned in class. It'll be this weekend. Can you come?"

Bonnie's face was stricken and Miles made that annoying stifled sound that he'd so perfected during book club. Bonnie finally said, "Of course, Miss Myrtle. I'll be there."

Miles pulled the car in front of Myrtle's house and said dryly, "You seem to be a destination now."

There were cars stopped in front of Myrtle's house and people taking pictures with their phones. She said, "Well, of *course*. These people must recognize great art when they see it. I'll have to tell Sam that he's getting some local attention and recognition." She snapped her fingers. "You know, he should have put a little sign in the yard with his name on it. As a signature. I'll have to make sure he does that."

Miles said, "And you really think this is going to prompt Red into action?"

"If this won't, nothing will. Besides, it'll be something to talk about at my dinner party if the yard hasn't been mowed by then."

The rest of the evening was quiet. Myrtle fixed herself breakfast for dinner (a favorite of hers) and settled down to work the crossword puzzle. There was a knock on her door around eight o'clock and she smiled to herself. It must be Red.

It was indeed Red. He looked more annoyed than he usually did.

"What's going on in your front yard?" he asked, hands on his hips.

"Well, that's a sad story. You see, my yardman's lawnmower became disabled and my son hasn't replaced it yet," said Myrtle, sitting back down in her armchair.

"You know what I mean," said Red with a long-suffering sigh.

"Oh. You mean the *art* that's in the middle of the wilderness. That was a brainchild of Elaine's very talented art student, Sam," said Myrtle. "Don't you love it?"

"It's very whimsical," said Red between gritted teeth.

"Yes, isn't it?"

"And I hate whimsical," said Red.

"Don't be such a grouch. But I'm glad you're here, Red. Any news on the case?" asked Myrtle.

Red's eyes narrowed. "Like I'm going to provide you with anything for you to stick in the newspaper."

"I promise that whatever you tell me in confidence won't go into the paper," said Myrtle, crossing her heart.

"All I can tell you is the information we *don't* have. We don't have witnesses. We don't have any helpful security camera footage. We don't have a very obvious motive except that Chester wasn't particularly well-liked," said Red with a sigh.

"Are you certain that it's someone in the cooking class?" asked Myrtle.

"It's either a student in the class, the teacher, or the custodian. There simply wasn't enough time for someone else to attack Chester. No one else would know exactly when the class was finished because that wasn't something that was published online in the course description. I suppose we can eliminate you and Miles," said Red dryly.

"And Wanda," reminded Myrtle.

"Considering you were with Wanda or with Chester the whole time, I think we can safely strike her off the list," agreed Red.

"Do we know when Chester's funeral is?" asked Myrtle.

"Forensics has finished with the body and it's being released to the family tomorrow. My understanding from his niece is that they'll have a graveside service in a couple of days," said Red.

"I'll be sure to pay my respects," said Myrtle.

Red gave her a stern look. "Now, Mama. You were hardly close, personal friends with Chester Struby."

"I *should* pay my respects. After all, I was Chester's teacher."

"Near the dawn of time," said Red.

"*And* I was his partner in the cooking class," said Myrtle.

"I can't keep you away from there; experience tells me that. But *my* experience tells me that our friendly local murderers like showing up at their victim's funerals. Make sure Miles is with you, and be careful," said Red.

"Naturally," said Myrtle rather huffily.

"And don't be nosy."

"Of *course not*." Myrtle was now desperate to move on to other subjects since Red was likely to soon start extolling the virtues of Greener Pastures retirement home. "What's the word on the mower?"

"Well that's the main reason I wanted to stick my head in before you started trying to fall asleep. I ran by the shop and they were completely out of the type of mower that I wanted," said Red.

"What type of mower was that? A cheap mower?"

"No, a mower that was reliable and that wouldn't break in a year. The last thing I want is for us to be in this same situation this time next year," said Red.

"That's one thing we can agree on, at least," said Myrtle. "When are they supposed to get one in? I'm having a dinner party here, you know."

Red looked wary at the mention of the dinner party. "They're having to order one and said it would take five to ten business days."

"Ten business days is half a month away!"

"Not much we can do about that, Mama. And now, I need to go home and try to get some sleep. You should do the same." Red seemed to be in a rush to get out of there.

Myrtle said, "Monday night, Red. That's the date of the dinner party and you're invited."

Red sighed. "Let me check in with Elaine, since she's the one who keeps the calendar. I'll have to let you know. Besides, with this case, I'm working all sorts of odd hours."

Myrtle thought about letting him know that most of his suspects would probably be there. But then she thought twice and said nothing.

The next day passed by unremarkably. Cooking class covered desserts, and somehow Miles always managed to have a leading role in whatever it was that they were making. Hattie had been in class, but she arrived late and left early, and Myrtle and Miles had no opportunity to speak with her at all. Later that afternoon, Myrtle had a visit from Elaine and Jack. Elaine, unlike her husband, had been very excited about Myrtle's yard and Sam's artistic talent. Myrtle had the feeling that Sam could have colored paint-by-numbers in Myrtle's yard and Elaine would have been just as convinced of his genius.

Myrtle had wanted to make a sympathy casserole for Hattie and drop it by her house as an excuse to talk with her. But when she was poring over her cookbooks and calling Miles on the phone, he made it clear that he did *not* feel like doing any murder investigating whatsoever. His allergies were acting up and he had a terrible headache. Myrtle offered to come by and cook dinner for him and he hastily said that he'd picked up some food from the deli and didn't need a thing.

The next day was another cooking class, and in this one Myrtle was too distracted to really pay any attention at all. She ended up putting salt instead of sugar into one dish and overcooked another.

Miles said in a low voice, "Sure you're ready for the dinner party?"

"Of course I am," she snapped. "I won't be distracted at all tomorrow."

"Even while preparing several dishes at the same time?" asked Miles doubtfully.

"I'm excellent at multitasking," said Myrtle.

Miles said, "I suppose we're going to Chester's funeral this afternoon?"

"That's right. We'll need to leave class a few minutes early, but I hardly think that's going to be a problem, under the circumstances," said Myrtle.

In fact, it was Louvenia who sped through the material and the dishes and said, "We're finishing up early today so that those of us who are interested in attending Chester's funeral can be there. Hattie emailed me to say that she was missing class today to prepare for the funeral. It's a graveside service at Grace Hill cemetery."

Myrtle leaned over to Miles. "We should go there directly from here. It's a shorter distance from here than from home."

Miles nodded, but looked morose at spending his afternoon at the graveyard.

Miles drove through Grace Hill cemetery's old iron gates, following the funeral home signs directing them to the "Struby service." He drove past ancient moss-covered stones and new markers. "I wonder how someone like Hattie was able to manage funeral preparations. That could hardly be something that someone her age is used to doing."

"The funeral home walks you through it," said Myrtle with a shrug. "All she'd have to do is speak to Chester's minister and he'd probably help with the rest of it. Although she's probably been to more funerals than you think. She's Chester's only living relative, remember?"

Miles said, "She'll probably be glad to see us there, then. There wouldn't be any other family in attendance, after all."

Myrtle squinted through the windshield, leaning forward in her seatbelt. "Is *that* Chester's service?"

Miles, who'd been driving very slowly down the winding road through the cemetery, paused. "I'm very much afraid it is. Can we turn around and leave? No one has probably spotted us yet. Or we could make the excuse that my headache has returned. As a matter of fact, I think my headache *has* returned."

Myrtle said, "Miles, this is our best chance to talk to Hattie. We're *not* leaving."

Miles waved wildly at the scene ahead of them. "But ... that!"

"That" was a voluminous black tulle tent over the graveside seating that replaced the normal funeral home tents. The folding chairs underneath the tent had black covers on them. Hattie was wearing a large black hat with a veil and an unusual and convoluted black dress that exposed her multitudinous tattoos. Instead of the meager scattering of people that Chester had predicted, there were crowds of people thronging around the grave site. Some looked as if they had worked for Chester's construction company and some were obviously friends of Hattie's. Hattie's friends were wearing very unusual black clothing and black hats and the women were wearing black lipstick. The construction workers stared outright at Hattie's friends as if they'd just landed from another planet.

Miles's mind was evidently following the same train of thought. "Where did Hattie's friends *come* from? I've never seen people like that in Bradley, North Carolina. And ... is that music I hear?" He cautiously rolled down the windows halfway as if whatever was happening at Chester's grave might be contagious.

The music was electronic, and sounded very modern, loud, and European.

"That's not *Amazing Grace*," said Miles.

"Well apparently *Amazing Grace* didn't make it onto Hattie's playlist for her uncle's funeral. I'll make sure it's on yours, though, since you seem so concerned," said Myrtle.

"If I predecease you," said Miles. "Which, considering our relative ages, might be doubtful."

Myrtle raised her eyebrows. "Women live longer than men. Besides, you're in danger, remember?"

Miles looked even glummer. "Don't remind me. Really, Myrtle, do we have to go? I have the feeling that we're not going to be able to talk to Hattie at all with this crowd of people here."

"We do. We must. Besides, it's our opportunity to experience our first truly avant-garde funeral."

"With any luck, our *only* opportunity," said Miles.

Chapter Thirteen

They stood at the very back of the assembled mourners. The funeral, although odd, was remarkably short, which won it some points in Myrtle's point of view. Myrtle attended many funerals that had dragged on well over an hour. There was no minister present; instead, there were eulogies given. Some of the eulogies were clearly planned with nervous speakers holding a script in front of them. Some of them were obviously written on the spur of the moment. Both Chester's associates from the construction industry and Hattie's unusual friends spoke. But Hattie's friends all prefaced their eulogies with: "I didn't really know Chester Struby, but ..."

Miles looked scandalized. He whispered, "No minister? No *ashes to ashes and dust to dust*?"

"Really, Miles. I'm now getting a very clear picture of what your own service will look like. What I think is, that the lack of a minister and the very unusual service says a lot about Hattie."

"It says that she's a strange young woman."

Myrtle shook her head. "It says more than that. Consider this—is this the type of service that *Chester* would have chosen for himself?"

"Absolutely not. He'd have had a traditional service with traditional hymns," said Miles.

"Right, of course he wouldn't have wanted a funeral service like this. This means the service is all about *Hattie* and what Hattie wants. I think she must be a very self-centered person," said Myrtle.

Miles said slowly in a low voice, "And if she's so self-centered, maybe she would even murder if it were in her own self-interest."

"Exactly," said Myrtle. She looked across the throng and saw Red there. He wasn't in uniform, but he was clearly on duty and watching everyone closely. Unfortunately, out of the cooking class, only Felix Todd was there. He wore a dark suit and was immaculately groomed, as usual. His eulogy for Chester hit the perfect notes of humor and regret and had everyone both laughing and wiping tears from their eyes.

"He's really something," said Miles.

"He's something, all right," agreed Myrtle. "I think he waited until no one else was walking up to make a eulogy. He wanted his to be the grand finale."

"Well, he *is* a politician." Miles paused. "I think it's over."

It was over, and Hattie disappeared into a throng of people wanting to extend their sympathy. Miles said grouchily, "This was what I was afraid of."

They took seats under the diaphanous tulle tent to wait for the crowd to disperse. Finally, Hattie had only a few people to speak with.

"She's probably going to bolt out of here as soon as she can," said Miles.

"Not without her purse," said Myrtle triumphantly holding up the small object.

Miles's eyes widened. "You took her purse?"

"I didn't *take* it. I'm *watching* it for her," said Myrtle.

"You think people steal purses at funeral services?"

"You just never know," said Myrtle. She patted the purse protectively.

Miles stifled a yawn, looking bored as they waited. Then he said, "Myrtle. What on earth are those things over there?"

Myrtle peered across at several canvases on stands that had been blocked by the crowd when they'd been standing. "Those appear to be works of art."

Miles stared at them, a horrified look on his face. "This isn't a gallery or a show. This is a funeral!"

Myrtle tilted her head to one side. "Look at them more closely. I think they're portraits."

Miles gawked at them. "Surely not."

"Yes. Yes, I think they are. That black thing there on the one painting? That's his nose," said Myrtle.

"*Whose* nose? That couldn't be Chester, surely."

"I believe it is," said Myrtle thoughtfully. "Although I'm not sure what Hattie is trying to say with it. As a matter of fact, I think they're *all* of Chester. I just can't tell if she used all that black because it's clearly her favorite color, or whether she used it because she didn't like her uncle all that much."

Miles said, "Shh. I think she's finally coming our way."

Hattie's face registered surprise. "Oh, hello. I didn't know you two were here. That was nice of you to come. Did you know my uncle outside of the cooking class?"

Myrtle said, "I taught Chester, actually. And we both wanted to come and pay our respects. We're so sorry for what happened."

Hattie's face changed to that polite, funeral face, and she came out quickly with a brusque, "Thanks. I'm sorry, too. It was a terrible tragedy." She watched as the funeral home director started packing things up.

Miles said, "It was. But you held a nice service—a nice testament to Chester's life." He somehow managed to say this earnestly. Myrtle decided that he was a better actor than she realized.

Hattie gave a short laugh. "Thanks. He'd have hated it, of course. Maybe not all the eulogies—he'd have loved those. But the rest of it wasn't something he'd have chosen. I couldn't have handled not putting my own stamp on the funeral, though."

Myrtle said quickly before the funeral home director got into earshot, "I wanted to ask you about Monday. The day Chester ... passed."

Hattie's eyes narrowed. "You mean the day he was murdered."

"Yes. That's right. You see, Miles and I have been so completely unsettled by this." She gestured to Miles, who did his best to look unsettled. "Imagine something like that happening at the community college and at a continuing education class! I think of schools as the safest places in the world, coming from an academic background."

Hattie said, "Sometimes no place is really safe. Not for some people."

Myrtle said, "So you think that it's something that Chester may have unwittingly brought on himself?"

"It makes me sound cruel, but yes. I loved my uncle, even though we didn't have a lot in common. When I lost my parents, he stepped in and took on their role with no questions asked. Even though he had no kids of his own and didn't really know what he was doing, he still did his best. I couldn't pay him back, but when he wanted to do things—like this cooking class—with me, I went along with it," said Hattie.

Miles frowned. "He sounds like a very caring person. Not a usual trait for a murder victim."

"And it's true—he was a kind, loving, flawed man who tried very hard to do the right thing. Some of the time. The rest of the time he was a ruthless businessman and a hard-driving construction company owner who frequently drank too much and got into fights. He was *both* of those things," said Hattie.

"Where were you when Chester was murdered?" asked Myrtle. "Didn't you ride together to the class?"

Hattie sighed. "No, we didn't, and I feel very guilty about it now. Chester sometimes could be really poky and I had plans for the rest of the afternoon. I told him I'd drive myself and meet him there at the class. After class, he was talking with people and I didn't really feel like hanging out. No offense," she said quickly.

"Oh, we didn't want to hang out, either," said Miles.

"No, we left right away. And you did the same? That is, you left the campus immediately?"

"That's right," said Hattie calmly. "I had no idea that anything had happened until I got a visit from the police."

Miles said, "It must have been a huge shock for you."

Hattie shrugged. "It was and it wasn't. Like I was saying, I knew my uncle had enemies."

Myrtle raised her eyebrows, "*Enemies* is a strong word. I thought you were merely talking about people he'd rubbed the wrong way in the business world."

"Look, I liked my uncle, okay? But I wasn't blind. He was a tough man and he could be cruel. I tried to tell the cops what I knew, but it wasn't a lot. I hardly knew anybody in that cooking class," said Hattie.

Myrtle said, "So you knew *somebody* in there? Who do you think could be responsible for this?"

Hattie held out her hands in front of her impatiently. "Amos, of course."

Miles said, "Amos? The custodian?"

"That's right. The janitor. Chester told me that he'd seen him as soon as he'd walked into the building," said Hattie.

Myrtle said slowly, "And Chester was the first student there, so that makes sense. Did he say anything else about him?"

"Oh, he said plenty during our break. I guess Amos was surprised to see him when he arrived that morning and walked over to give him a piece of his mind. Chester said Amos blamed him for ruining his career in construction and forcing him to work as a custodian." Hattie snorted. "As if Chester had something to do with Amos's job choice."

Myrtle said, "He meant that Chester had taken away his choices. That he couldn't be in construction anymore and was forced to work other jobs."

Hattie said, "Whatever. All I know is that Chester told me that Amos had an accident on the job and it kept him from being able to work. And that Amos was still really furious. So what do *you* think? It sounds to me like Amos had motivation and plenty of opportunity. He was in the building and would have been able to see who was coming and going and when the class had come to a close."

Myrtle nodded. "I'm sure the police consider him a suspect." She paused. "And now what are you going to do? Are there many of Chester's affairs you need to settle?"

Hattie's eyes gleamed. "Now I'm running a construction company. I'll be figuring out the ropes."

Miles said, "He left you the company?"

"You sound surprised," said Hattie with a hard laugh. "Because I'm a woman? A woman working in construction?"

"Not at all," said Miles coolly. "I'm surprised because you're so young and likely inexperienced."

Myrtle hid a smile. Her sidekick did not like to have people make assumptions about him.

Hattie said, "Oh. Well he didn't have anybody else to leave it to and he obviously wasn't expecting to die so soon. I guess he thought that he'd have lots of time to show me how things in the office worked."

Myrtle said, "Apparently Louvenia knows how things in the office worked."

Hattie looked confused. "Louvenia? From the cooking class?"

"She used to work for your uncle," said Myrtle.

Hattie's eyebrows knitted together. "Oh. I knew they seemed to know each other, but I didn't know why."

"Did you not spend much time in your uncle's office?" asked Miles.

"I spent time there. But I didn't pay a lot of attention to the people working there," said Hattie. "So, Chester knew someone else in the class. Besides Felix, I mean."

"He was also in school with Bonnie," said Myrtle.

Hattie frowned. "You're saying he knew everybody in class? Including you and Miles?"

Miles said quickly, "He didn't know me."

"What were your thoughts on Felix?" asked Myrtle.

Hattie shrugged. "Well, he gave a good eulogy. But I guess politicians are good at public speaking."

Miles said, "They were friends, right? From back in school?"

Hattie gave that hard laugh again. "Kind of weird friends. The kind of friends who don't always get along. I know Felix was mad at Chester lately. Chester wouldn't put one of those yard sign things in his yard and that made him upset."

"Yard sign things?" asked Myrtle.

"You know—the signs you put in your yard to show your support for somebody running for office. Felix is running and he expected Chester to put a sign in his yard. Chester's house and yard are huge," said Hattie.

Myrtle said, "Oh, I remember. And in an area where a lot of cars drive by—a very prominent location for a yard sign. Chester wasn't supporting Felix in the race?"

Hattie said, "Chester wasn't supporting *anybody* in the race. Chester wasn't a very political guy. Anyway, he didn't want a sign in his yard."

Myrtle and Miles looked at each other. Maybe Chester wasn't outwardly political, but he cared about who he could manipulate. Perhaps he thought Felix wasn't someone he could easily railroad.

Hattie misinterpreted the look. "But they made up, you know. That's why Felix was here today. Look, I really need to go take this stuff down before it rains. Do you mind?"

"Not at all," said Myrtle. "Oh. I almost forgot ... can you come to my dinner party Monday evening? It'll be coffee and dinner. The cooking class will be there, among others, and I can practice some of what we learned in school. I decided not to have it over the weekend since everyone always has plans."

Hattie looked as if the last thing in the world she wanted to do was to go to Myrtle's dinner party. But she was apparently knocked off guard and didn't have a ready excuse.

"Perfect!" said Myrtle, beaming. "And I've got your email address from our group emails. I'll send everyone my address. We'll have so much fun!"

Hattie gave her a weak smile.

Chapter Fourteen

At cooking class on Monday morning, Louvenia covered a very fancy couple of entrees. Miles said under his breath, "These meals are probably the bulk of the tuition. I'd rather know how to make a better omelet."

"Shh. We can't serve omelets at dinner parties," said Myrtle.

"I'm not sure I'd want to serve *this* at a dinner party," said Miles. "The sauce is a really odd, muddy color."

Myrtle frowned at it. "I'm sure I followed the directions exactly. It just looks like gravy to me."

"That's exactly the problem. It's not *supposed* to look like gravy. It's supposed to be a clear sauce," said Miles. "It's not very appetizing looking. Let's not put it on the meat."

"But then the meat won't be tender. The recipe said to put the sauce on the chicken, Miles."

"Only if the sauce looks like the sauce in the book," said Miles stubbornly.

In the end, Myrtle put the sauce on the chicken. And, whatever the sauce was, it made the chicken inedible in the end.

When it had come out of the oven and he'd plated it, Miles said sadly, "And we can't even enjoy the fruits of our labors now."

"Sure we can! Just scrape it off, Miles. It's fine," said Myrtle.

"All right everyone," sang out Louvenia. "It's time for our break. Let's put any uneaten food into the refrigerator."

"Saved by the bell," said Miles. He hastily wrapped up the chicken and vegetables and put them out of sight in the fridge.

Bonnie hurried out of the class.

"I think she's avoiding us," said Miles.

"Of course not. We're perfectly pleasant and fun to be with. She's probably got an important phone call to make. Like Felix." Myrtle nodded at Felix as he gave them his toothiest smile and punched in some numbers on his cell phone. Hattie, back at the class, gave them a tight smile and headed outdoors.

Amos, the custodian, was carrying a broom and walked up to them. "How are things going?" he asked. "No more trouble in the class?"

"No more like the trouble we *were* having," said Myrtle.

Amos said, "Did y'all go to the funeral Friday?" His face couldn't hide his curiosity.

"We did," said Myrtle nodding.

Amos said, "Yeah, I was working. Although I wouldn't have wanted to go anyway, you know. How did it go?"

Miles said, "It was very interesting."

Myrtle rolled her eyes. "Hattie made the arrangements—the young woman in our cooking class who's Chester's niece. She's very artistic and the service was, too. It was well-attended."

"That's good." Amos shuffled his feet a little. "How is your class going?" he asked. "I love food and cooking. Wish I could do more of it."

Miles said dryly, "Cooking isn't all it's cracked up to be."

Myrtle gave him a look. "It's fun. And we've learned a lot. I'm even hosting a dinner party and coffee tonight for members of the class to demonstrate what I've learned."

"The class is coming?" asked Amos, looking suddenly interested.

"Well, they're invited. No one has turned me *down*."

"It sounds really nice," said Amos a bit wistfully. "I'd love to see what you've learned so far."

"Really? Well, if you give me your email address, I'll send you an invitation. We'll have coffee beforehand and then dinner."

Amos grinned at her. "I'd love that, thanks. I don't have anything else going on."

Miles put a hand to his forehead and gently rubbed.

After class ended, Miles was still dwelling on Myrtle's party. "This is starting to sound like a big crowd of people, Myrtle."

"Oh, I don't think so. I've really only invited the people in our cooking class."

"That's not really true. Maybe those are the people who stand out to you the most because you wanted to make sure all the suspects were invited. But you also casually mentioned it in conversation at the book club."

Myrtle frowned. "Probably no one was listening."

"I think you've casually invited quite a few people in passing. And I heard you mention it a couple of times when you got phone calls."

Myrtle said irritably, "All right, all right. Maybe I've extended more invitations than I realized. I'm sure not *all* of them are coming. Even if they *were* all coming, I'm sure that I could handle it. I've hosted large gatherings before. Bonkers, for one."

"Bunco. And you didn't have to serve a full meal," said Miles.

Myrtle thought this over for a minute. "Maybe I do need some kitchen help for the night. A sous-chef. Or even a scullery maid." She studied Miles.

"Oh no. No. I don't want any connection with this meal," said Miles, raising his hands in protest. "Nothing that can be traced back to me."

"For heaven's sake, Miles! You act as though you're trying not to leave evidence at a crime scene."

Miles gave her a wary look.

"All right. I guess I could call Puddin up. Although she was just at my house, which means she won't want to come," said Myrtle.

"Maybe you could tempt her by telling her you bought new household cleaners. That always seems to pique her interest," said Miles.

"That's true. Although usually I don't have a hard time getting her to come over if I tell her it's a party. Even though it means she spends a lot of surreptitious time at the drinks table," said Myrtle.

"Is Puddin helpful in the kitchen, though?" asked Miles doubtfully.

"Well, the words *helpful* and *Puddin* are rarely mentioned in the same breath. I suppose she'd do all right as a dishwasher or pot-stirrer," said Myrtle. She paused. "How much food do you think I need?"

Miles thought this through. "I guess it would be much worse to have too little food than to have too much food."

"I could always freeze the leftovers. Or send them home with guests. All right. Could you take me to the store? I feel as though I should really stock up, just in case," said Myrtle.

"Are you sure you can afford it? That meal we cooked today was very expensive," said Miles.

"I don't think I'm doing the one from today. The sauce was definitely odd. No, I think I'll do the one we cooked on the second or third day of class. That was prettier and the ingredients weren't quite as exotic. Can we go now?" asked Myrtle.

"Now? But you don't have your shopping list, do you?"

Myrtle pulled the folded-up recipe out of her pocketbook. "We'll just go off the recipe. And I've got the recipes for the sides and dessert, too. Oh, and the hors d'oeuvres, as well." She continued pulling folded up sheets out of the purse.

"Sounds like you have it covered then. Except for the drinks, of course," said Miles.

Myrtle said, "I don't fancy having drunken murder suspects at my house. I'll serve iced tea and just offer everyone one glass of wine for dinner. That should work."

Miles looked gloomy. "No alcohol? But alcohol makes the meal more palatable."

Myrtle squinted suspiciously at him. "Are you implying that my meal won't be palatable without copious alcohol?"

"No, no. I'm just saying that it makes *every* meal better," said Miles in a rush. "Besides, it will help me keep my mind off the fact that I'm in danger."

"You should stop brooding over that. I've been in danger for ages and I'm still around to tell the tale," said Myrtle. "To the store!"

The trip to the store was something of an adventure.

Myrtle said, "What on earth are chia seeds? I don't remember those being part of the recipes."

Miles sighed. "You probably didn't include them."

"Well, everything that I made tasted fine. I'm going to skip them. And ... quinoa? Really? Did we use quinoa in our class?"

"*I* did," said Miles tersely. "What *you* might or might not have done is anyone's guess."

Myrtle said, "Why don't I see it here with the rice? It's a rice-type thing."

"Because we're in a small grocery store in a remote area of North Carolina," said Miles.

Myrtle started walking toward customer service. "Maybe they keep it in a strange place here. They *should* have it. It's mainstream now. You keep working through those recipes."

Miles sighed and peered at one of the recipes.

A few minutes later, Myrtle returned, looking irritated. "They'd never even *heard* of quinoa in customer service. They acted as though I'd made it up to make them look bad. Are you making headway with the ingredients?"

Miles grunted. "The print is really small on these."

"I think she was trying to save money on ink or something." Myrtle's pocketbook started making a ringing sound. "Who on earth is this?" She fished it out and shooed Miles on to keep shopping. "Dusty? *You're* calling *me*? Are pigs flying?"

Dusty sounded grouchy. "Miz Myrtle, yer yard looks awful."

"Well, it does and it doesn't. If you're looking at it strictly from a horticultural or landscaping sense, yes. But if you're observing it through an artistic lens, then that's something else."

Dusty was quiet for a minute, as if trying to digest Myrtle's last statement. Then he said, "Don't know what yer talkin' about, but yer yard is bad. Real bad. An' people know I cut it."

"Ah. You're looking at it purely as poor advertising that could be detrimental to your business. I see. Pity you don't look at it that way on a weekly basis," said Myrtle tartly.

"It don't never look *this* bad. You asked Red 'bout that mower?" asked Dusty.

"I have inquired at length about it, yes. Red informs me that he wants a particular type of mower that's well-reviewed and supposed to be reliable and relatively affordable. Unfortunately, those mowers were out of stock at the shop, so they're on order. He promises it will be in soon. What are you doing in the meantime? How are you able to still work?" Myrtle had a jolt of anxiety. What if Dusty went bankrupt in the interim and had to take another job? She couldn't afford any of the other yardmen in town.

"Aw, I'm borrowin' a mower from Tiny. He collects 'em."

Tiny was an ineptly-nicknamed 300-pound yardman who stood at 6'7".

"It figures that Tiny would have odd hobbies like collecting yard equipment. But it's nice for him to lend one out to you," said Myrtle. She slowly followed Miles as he walked to another aisle of the store.

"Oh, he ain't really *lending* it. I'm renting it," said Dusty sourly. "Anyhow, I've got one. Want me to come mow?"

"Not right now, no. You wouldn't be able to do it around the gnome art out there. Besides, if we cleaned up the yard, the art wouldn't make sense anymore," said Myrtle.

Dusty snorted as if the art didn't make sense *now*.

"Plus the fact that it acts as a reminder to Red to keep checking on the mower and to pick it up as soon as it comes into the store," said Myrtle. "But I'm glad you called me. I wanted to ask Puddin something."

"Her was just there at yer house," said Dusty. "An' she says them exercises you give her made her neck have a crick."

"I doubt she's even tried them. Anyway, I know she was just here, but I need her again. It's for a party I'm having tonight. She's pretty good in the kitchen, isn't she?"

Dusty grunted as if he didn't want to comment on Puddin's abilities one way or the other.

"Anyway, can you put her on?" asked Myrtle impatiently.

"I done cleaned," said Puddin plaintively when she picked up.

"Well, I suppose you did your best. It's fairly clean, I'll agree. But that's not why I need you. I'm having a dinner party tonight and I could use your help. You've helped me in the past when I've entertained," said Myrtle.

Miles was staring at a wall of spices with a very confused expression on his face.

Puddin said, sounding a bit more interested, "What, like freshening up drinks and whatnot?"

"Well, I was thinking more of giving me a hand in the kitchen," said Myrtle.

"What? With them dishes?" Puddin sounded horrified.

"It's not like you're scrubbing them by hand, you know. I've got a dishwasher. Besides, you can also help me with stirring, taking things out of the oven, chopping vegetables, that kind of thing. I just need an extra set of hands, that's all," said Myrtle. She rolled her eyes at Miles and he smiled. Getting Puddin to do anything was exhausting for the one trying to get it done.

"On a Monday night, hm. Well, that's when Dusty and me goes out," said Puddin, sounding sly.

Myrtle sighed. This is where the extortion came in. She was sure that probably the last time Dusty had taken Puddin out, there had been golden arches and hamburgers involved instead of something special.

"The dinner party is already taking a toll on my wallet," said Myrtle, grimacing at the grocery cart as Miles threw in a few more bottles of spices.

Puddin simply waited, holding her tongue on the other end of the line.

"I suppose I could spare an extra fifteen dollars onto your usual hourly fee," said Myrtle grudgingly. She followed Miles to another aisle of the store.

"What time should I be there?" asked Puddin.

"Let's say five o'clock. No, make it four thirty. And wear something nice, please, especially since you might help me serve the guests."

"Something nice?" asked Puddin.

"Maybe a black tee shirt and black pants? Just don't try to stand out," said Myrtle.

She rang off and said, "Are you sure I need all those spices? Spices are exorbitant. I do have garlic and onion powder, you know."

Miles said, "I'm sure you do. But do you have caraway seeds? Or Marjoram?"

"What on earth are those? Are you sure we cooked with those spices in class?" demanded Myrtle.

"I think the ingredients didn't make much of an impression on you because you simply had to reach across, check the label, and use one of the class's communal spice bottles. I promise you that these ingredients were in there," said Miles.

"Well, pooh. I guess I'll have to get them then. Are we almost done here?"

"I think we're only three-fourths of the way done," said Miles.

Myrtle groaned.

It was good that Miles was there to give her a hand. Even between the two of them, it took forever to unload the groceries.

Miles seemed eager to get out of there.

"Make sure you're here early tonight," said Myrtle as he started hurrying toward her front door. "Maybe you can give me a hand, too."

"Myrtle, I don't think I can make it early. But I'll be here as soon as I can. After all, I'm not *giving* the dinner. I'm just *attending*," said Miles, leaving before Myrtle could dispute the point.

Chapter Fifteen

That afternoon was hectic. Myrtle sent a follow-up reminder to everyone she *wanted* to attend and skipped the ones that she hoped had forgotten her informal invitation. She pulled out more chairs and borrowed card tables and tablecloths from various friends to have enough table space. Then she set up a modest bar in one corner with her sherry glasses, which were tiny. With any luck, everyone would have just one very small drink.

Myrtle then studied the recipes. She figured she could make some of the dishes in advance instead of trying to tackle them all at once and under pressure. Pasha, swishing her tail, watched from a window sill as Myrtle chopped potatoes and rinsed green beans.

The doorbell rang at five o'clock and she opened it to see Puddin there.

"Good," said Myrtle. "I've got some things for you to do."

Puddin raised a hand. "Since you was fussin' at me about the cleaners, I done brought one of mine. You'll love the way it smells."

"I'm sure I will, Puddin, but we don't have time for that now. There's lots to do."

Puddin raised her chin. "But I want to show you. It'll just take a second. Smells good."

"Not now! I need you to focus on other things," said Myrtle.

She led Puddin into the kitchen, pointing at a pot that needed stirring. Puddin, however, seemed to be moving at a turtle's pace. "Look, we need to hurry. People will probably be arriving in an hour."

Puddin frowned at Myrtle. "Then they'll drink. That's what they do."

"Not here they won't. After spending so much on the meal, I didn't want to buy a bunch of alcohol," said Myrtle briskly. "They'll have coffee when they arrive and then water and one glass of wine with dinner."

"Why don't you just tell them to BYOB?" Puddin started resentfully stirring a bubbling sauce on Myrtle's stove.

"I don't think that would be good hostess behavior," said Myrtle. She glanced over at the pot. "Why is stirring that sauce so laborious? You act as if you're barely able to move the spoon."

"That's because I'm barely able to move the spoon," answered Puddin tartly.

Myrtle frowned before shrugging. "Oh well. I guess it's the type of thing that just thickens as you stir it. Now let's see. I need to get a batch of vegetables cooked. Where's my cutting board?"

Puddin wrenched the spoon around another rotation, panting a bit as she did.

"Takes a while to boil the water, if yer boilin' veggies," said Puddin. "Want me to get that started?"

Clearly Puddin was trying to get out of stirring duty. "No, no. I'll turn on the boiler and put a pot of water on," said Myrtle. She did, and then put her hands on her hips. "Where *is* that cutting board?"

"Is it that scrap over there?" asked Puddin, nodding at a plastic rectangle partially covered by grocery bags.

"Oh yes. That's right." Myrtle set up the cutting board on the stove so that she could cut vegetables and toss them right into the pot of water. "This is called 'kitchen efficiency,' Puddin.

Louvenia taught us all sorts of helpful tips for speeding up the cooking process. I have a central area to throw away trash, too. It makes so much sense."

Puddin grunted. "Miz Myrtle? Ain't this sauce done yet? I don't think it can be stirred no more."

"I suppose so. It's pretty thick." Myrtle chopped up some potatoes with a bit of difficulty.

"What's the sauce for?" asked Puddin.

"It's supposed to go on the chicken."

Puddin looked doubtfully in the pot. "Don't look like a sauce."

"Of course it does! What do *you* think it looks like?"

Puddin said, "A spread. Kind of a thick peanut butter."

Myrtle said, "Well, I followed the directions exactly, Puddin. It should be fine." Her nose wrinkled and she frowned.

Puddin frowned, too. "Smell somethin' funny?"

Myrtle stopped chopping and looked around the room. "Isn't that a burning smell?"

"Like bad burning. Like electric burning," said Puddin, squinting suspiciously at the light switches and fixtures.

"This is no time for an electrical fire," said Myrtle, putting her hands on her hips. "My patience is really being tried today. Take that pot off the burner and let's check all the appliances. I certainly hope it's not the stove!"

Checking all the appliances and outlets took five minutes. By the end of the five minutes, the smell had intensified into a sickly-sweet burning.

"Where on earth is that coming from?" demanded Myrtle.

There was a knock on the door and Myrtle said, "Go get that, Puddin, would you?"

Puddin slouched off to answer the door and returned with an anxious-looking Miles.

"I thought you had something to do," said Myrtle.

"Well, I did. But then I thought it might be best if I checked in here," said Miles. "What's burning?"

"A good question! Puddin and I have been knocking ourselves out trying to figure out where the smell is coming from," said Myrtle.

Miles's eyebrows knitted. "Myrtle? What's that?"

"What's what?"

Miles pointed to the stove.

"They're *vegetables*, Miles. Chopped vegetables," said Myrtle, as if speaking to someone very young.

Miles said, "Yes. But the cutting board shouldn't be bubbling."

"What?" Myrtle flew over to the stove.

"Let's turn off the burner first," said Miles.

"But this wasn't the burner that was supposed to be on! It was supposed to be the back one!" said Myrtle.

"Apparently, the stove got the wrong message," said Miles.

He turned off the burner, found the heaviest-duty potholders he could find, and carefully lifted the melting plastic cutting board. The burner went with it, stuck to the underside of the board.

"Please turn on the exhaust hood," said Miles, coughing a bit.

"Oh, the fan? It hasn't worked in years," said Myrtle. "I usually just open windows."

"Please open windows," said Miles.

Myrtle and Puddin opened all the windows in the kitchen and then, at Miles's bequest, opened the windows in other rooms, too.

"Now I'm running behind," said Myrtle irritably. "I haven't even gotten the vegetables cut."

Miles said, "I smell something burning."

"That's already been established," said Myrtle.

"No, I smell something *else* burning," said Miles.

Myrtle gasped. "My hors d'oeuvres!"

The hors d'oeuvres were completely annihilated.

"Now what am I supposed to do?" demanded Myrtle of the universe.

Miles said, "I think I would go ahead and start making the main dishes. Not having an hors d'oeuvres is understandable, but not having an entrée is unforgivable."

"But I wanted to have them eat before the meal in case there wasn't enough food! And I wanted them to drink coffee before the meal to fill themselves up and so they wouldn't want alcohol. And we haven't even had time to make coffee!" said Myrtle.

Puddin said, "I'll make coffee. Better'n trying to spread the chicken with that sauce thing."

Miles said, "And I'll scrape plastic off the stove."

"I'm calling Elaine. I really did want everyone to have hors d'oeuvres," said Myrtle, still not wanting to let it go. She walked into the living room.

But Elaine hadn't been to the store in days. "Unless you want to serve cereal as an appetizer. That's all I've got. But I'll drop by some wine in a little bit. That should help to make things go smoother."

Myrtle said glumly, "Maybe with enough alcohol, they'll forget they're hungry." She hung up. Her nose wrinkled. Now something *else* smelled bad.

"What do I smell now?" bellowed Myrtle.

Puddin yelled back over the fan. "The new cleaning stuff. Told you it smelled good. I'm trying to cover up the burnin' smell."

Myrtle hurried into the kitchen where Miles was turning blue in his effort to hold his breath.

"It does *not* smell good, Puddin. It's far too strong. It smells like a pine forest on growth hormones!" said Myrtle.

"Or an institution," said Miles, gasping.

"Exactly!" said Myrtle. "My home smells like the DMV or the health department or something!"

Miles added, "If they'd had a fire."

Myrtle looked for more windows to open.

When she returned to the kitchen, Miles said, "Any updates on the hors d'oeuvres?"

"Elaine's cupboard is bare, apparently. Miles, you don't have anything at your house we can serve, do you?"

Miles shook his head. "I need to go to the store, too." He paused. "I hesitate to mention this as a remedy to your problem, but Erma Sherman always seems to have something to eat at her house."

"But that would mean *inviting* her," said Myrtle with a shudder.

"Not inviting her is probably a bad idea. She'll clearly see you're having a dinner party and when her feelings get hurt, she's impossible to deal with," said Miles.

Myrtle still stalled until Miles said, "I'll go over myself and ask her. And I'll invite her to come over." He glanced through the kitchen door at the tables in her living room. "Maybe she could even bring a chair or two."

Erma did want to come over. And she did have something to eat. Miles was back in a few minutes with a couple of chairs and Erma. She was wearing an ill-fitting floral dress and carried a tray of food. Myrtle gave her a tight smile and tried to be gracious over the bowls of nuts and crackers and cheese that Erma was carrying, although, they were not nearly as interesting as the fabulous hors d'oeuvres that she'd been planning on serving.

Erma said, "Now what can I do? I love to help in the kitchen! Except I can't help out if there is shellfish. I have a terrible allergy to shellfish and have the most disgusting reaction."

Puddin gave Myrtle an alarmed look and Myrtle quickly said to Erma, "Actually, everything in the kitchen is under control."

Miles snorted and Myrtle repeated firmly, "It's all under control. What you could do is to help me let people in. For some reason, even though people are *invited* to my house, they ring the bell and wait to be admitted."

"I don't do that," said Puddin, helpfully.

"But when you let yourself in, it's at times that I have no idea you're coming," said Myrtle in an irritable voice.

Erma said, "No worries, Myrtle! I will greet guests and make sure everyone has something to drink."

"Yes. And about that ... I'm wanting everyone to have a pre-dinner coffee. And probably a post-dinner coffee. And they can have as much sweet tea as they can possibly consume," said Myrtle.

Erma quickly translated this in her head. "So ... no alcohol?"

"Not immediately, no. With dinner."

Erma heaved a tremendous sigh and nodded.

Myrtle returned to the kitchen and got out her mixer. She glanced around. "Why are there never enough outlets in here?"

Puddin nodded toward the slow cooker. "What's in there?"

"That's mashed potatoes. I guess I could put the slow cooker in the oven and use that outlet for my mixer. It's a ceramic pot, after all." Myrtle took the pot out of the slow cooker and stuck it in the oven with the chicken.

Unfortunately, Myrtle soon discovered that the slow cooker's *top* had a plastic handle on it. A top which started burning and making that same distinctive smell. She took out the slow cooker and tried scraping the top of it to get the burned plastic off.

Pasha jumped in through the open kitchen window to see what was going on right as the doorbell rang.

"That witch-cat!" hissed Puddin. "Can't work with her!"

"Ignore her! That window needs to stay open to get rid of the burning smell!" Myrtle gave Miles a look as he snickered. "You can put yourself to use by seeing who's there at the door."

Miles peered out. "It's Louvenia."

"Oh good. Maybe she can give us a hand back here," said Myrtle.

"Well, right now Erma seems to be monopolizing her attention. And serving her coffee."

The doorbell rang again and Miles reported in. "Now Amos and Bonnie and Felix are here."

Myrtle frowned "Isn't it too early for everyone to be here?"

"No, they're right on time. In fact, they're a little late," said Miles. "But Erma is directing them to the nuts and cheeses and giving them all coffee."

Twenty-five minutes later, Myrtle said to Puddin, "I think this meal is as good as it's going to get."

Puddin looked doubtfully at the chicken and the vegetables.

"Could you go and get Louvenia? You know her, don't you? Ask her to come back here and make sure this is good to serve," said Myrtle.

Puddin sauntered out of the kitchen and returned a minute later, making a face. "She can't help."

Myrtle put her hands on her hips. "Why on earth not?"

"Her is drunk," said Puddin succinctly.

"What? How can she be drunk? Erma has been giving everyone coffee. Even Elaine hasn't come over yet with the wine," said Myrtle.

Puddin shrugged. "Drunk."

Miles intoned, "A crust eaten in peace is better than a banquet partaken in anxiety."

Myrtle glared at him. "Thanks a lot, Mr. Aesop. Sorry you're so ridden with anxiety that you can't weather a couple of minor dinner party mishaps. Although it *is* annoying about Louvenia.

She must have arrived here intoxicated, since she's only been given coffee here. How disappointing! All right, then, I guess we're ready to serve."

Myrtle and Puddin started helping plates and putting them on the table as Myrtle's guests took their seats. Myrtle saw with relief that her book club had apparently opted *not* to come. Only the cooking class members and Miles and Erma were there. Even Hattie had come, although she was wearing black lipstick and heavy black eyeshadow.

Louvenia did indeed seem intoxicated. She was laughing uproariously at something that Felix said to her and Felix gave Myrtle a wink. Puddin rolled her eyes and set down the chicken and vegetables with a clatter.

"Oh, my. This looks *delicioussss*!" slurred Louvenia loudly.

Everyone else was staring at their plates in discomfort. When Myrtle put Miles's plate in front of him, he said in a hushed voice, "Is the sauce supposed to stand on the chicken? I don't think I remember that in class."

"It's delicious," said Myrtle sourly. "Be sure to be a member of the clean plate club."

Amos was dressed neatly in a carefully pressed pair of dress pants and a button-down shirt with a tie. No one else was dressed nearly as nicely; except, of course, for Miles, who always dressed that way. Amos looked a little uncomfortable at being part of the group, but was making halting conversation with Bonnie.

If it was a little quiet in the room, Felix and Erma made up for it. Erma was giving a nonstop monologue about a wonderful dinner she'd had when she'd been an exchange student in France a million years ago (although she'd suffered some sort of terrible stomach flu afterward—she was sure it was in no way connected). And Felix was making Louvenia laugh so loudly that she wasn't able to even eat.

Pasha, tail twitching and ears back, watched them from the top of Myrtle's desk, at some distance away. And Puddin watched Pasha.

There was a tap on the front door and Myrtle frowned. "I thought everyone was here."

It was Elaine. "So sorry—I got caught up at home. Here's the wine. At least it's chilled." She leaned into the room and gave a cheery smile and wave. "Hi everybody! Wish I could stay, but I've got Jack with me."

Myrtle whispered to her, "Jack would be a vast improvement on Louvenia."

Elaine's eyebrows shot up as she glanced over at the table. She quickly continued, "Enjoy your meal. I brought some wine."

There was a cheer from behind Myrtle.

Everyone seemed eager to have wine and Myrtle and Puddin opened the bottles of wine and poured them.

Felix said in an earnest voice, "Miss Myrtle, thank you so much for this lovely meal and all the preparations for it. It was very kind of you to host us here."

Myrtle beamed at him. "You're very welcome. I thought, since the cooking class was teaching us some special occasion cooking, that it made sense to have everyone over for a special occasion."

She was finally able to take a seat, herself. Myrtle noticed that there seemed to be a lot of pushing food around on plates and a lot of wine drinking. She took a bite of the chicken with the sauce. She washed it down with some of her water. It appeared that there might have been too much flour in that sauce. She carefully scraped the sauce off and started in on the chicken.

It had fallen quiet again, minus Erma's medical monologue. Hattie said abruptly, "Miss Myrtle? Tell me about what was going on in your yard."

Everyone looked stricken, as if Myrtle's yard was some sort of terrible scar that shouldn't be mentioned in front of the person who had it.

"It's yard art," said Myrtle. "Isn't it brilliant? It's art of yard art."

"Art of yard art," said Hattie thoughtfully. "That's actually very, very interesting." She looked surprised as she said it.

"Sam Sinclair is the art student's name. I'm sure one day we'll have to pay gobs of money for his work," said Myrtle.

Hattie's gaze drifted over to the begging, leering gnome near Myrtle's desk. "Is that more of Sam's work?" she asked.

Myrtle frowned. She'd meant to move the gnome into another room. "No. No, that's Elaine's piece. She's experimenting with restoration."

The guests stared solemnly at the gnome, not sure what to say.

Bonnie spilled her wine on the table and looked at the spill sadly. "Oh no," she whispered.

Felix reached over to try to upright the wine glass and knocked his over in the process. He sighed. "Clumsy."

Amos leaped up beside Bonnie and started dabbing at the wine with his own napkin. "It's easy to do," he said kindly. "No use crying over spilt milk."

Miles stood and started collecting plates from the table to take to the kitchen.

Myrtle said, "Miles! They may not be finished eating."

"I am," said Hattie quickly. "It was ... very filling."

Felix leapt to his feet to help Miles. "Isn't it amazing how filling it was? A wonderful dinner, Myrtle."

Erma leaned over and said to Bonnie, "Just scrape that sauce off and it's much better."

Myrtle bristled. Clearly no one here recognized haute cuisine. Even if they'd been taught it in class.

Louvenia seemed to be commenting about the food, but her speech was so slurred that the words were unrecognizable. Felix said, "May I give you a hand, Louvenia?"

It was a good thing he did, because she would have fallen to the floor if he hadn't had an arm around her, supporting her.

"So dizzy," muttered Louvenia.

Felix said solicitously, "Would you like me to take you home, Louvenia?"

"Or you could put your feet up in my room," offered Myrtle.

"Not feeling so well," said Louvenia. "Head hurts. Home." She stumbled a bit and Felix pulled her back up.

Felix said, "I'll take you home, Louvenia. Then tomorrow maybe you can catch a ride with someone to come back and get your car."

Myrtle nodded. The last thing she wanted was for Louvenia to drive home from her house in that condition.

Felix said as he walked carefully out the door with Louvenia, "Thanks again, Miss Myrtle. Sorry I had to eat and run."

"Or just run," said Myrtle sourly under her breath to Miles as she helped him get the last of the plates. "I'm not sure he ate anything at all. It looked as if he were shoving food around on his plate. I'm certain he hid his chicken under his mashed potatoes. And where's that Puddin? I need her to start washing up and to serve some coffee!"

Hattie called from the living room, "I really have to get going, myself. I've got so much to do right now. Thanks, Miss Myrtle."

Bonnie and Amos also quickly left.

Myrtle put her hands on her hips. "Well, it hardly seems worth all the work. And I have all this leftover food! You'll have to take some to Dusty, Puddin."

"Dusty don't like burnt food," muttered Puddin.

"It isn't all burned. Oh, I guess I'll freeze some of the rest. What a pain, though," said Myrtle dejectedly.

Miles pushed his glasses up his nose. "You know, I think it went rather well."

"Did you? Were you paying attention?" asked Myrtle.

"No, I really do. There was still plenty of food to be had. No one seemed to notice the lack of wine. The conversation appeared to go well," enumerated Miles.

Myrtle said, "I suppose. Although I wasn't counting on my cooking class teacher to be intoxicated at dinner. And there was too *much* food to be had."

"I guess Erma's hors d'oeuvres filled everyone up," said Miles carefully.

Myrtle was about to rant about Erma's conversational topics when she stopped to peer more closely at Miles. "You're looking very tired."

"It's been a long week. But many hands make light work—I'll help you with the cleanup."

"No, no. You were a guest, the same as anyone else. And you also did a lot of cleaning before the party even started. No, you go home and get some sleep. Puddin and I will tackle this."

Puddin sighed.

Chapter Sixteen

Eventually, much of the mess was cleaned up and put away and Myrtle finally turned in. She managed to sleep this time, too, although she had nightmares about the scraped-off sauce growing and growing around the dining room table until she and the guests were barricaded in by it.

Miles called her as she was getting ready the next morning.

"I really don't feel like going to class this morning," he said. "I feel as if we just saw those people."

"We did just see them. Although I really didn't even have a chance to talk with any of them. Come on. We should go. We're practically at the end of the class," said Myrtle.

A few minutes later, Miles had picked her up and they were heading to the community college.

"I suspect that Louvenia isn't going to be her usual, chipper self in class today," said Miles dryly.

Myrtle nodded. "She'll be nursing a huge hangover. We'll probably get out of class early. I can't imagine what possessed her to arrive intoxicated to my dinner party."

Miles smirked and Myrtle gave him a sharp look. "No jokes about my cooking! Everything would have gone perfectly last night if I hadn't been distracted by having so many dishes to cook."

Miles said, "So you think she actually *arrived* drunk."

"Well, she couldn't have gotten drunk at *my* house unless she brought some sort of flask with her," said Myrtle. "Erma was serving everyone coffee when they came in, remember?"

After they'd arrived at the school and parked, they ascended the stairs.

"It's awfully quiet in here," said Miles.

"Then it's just as we said—Louvenia is probably keeping very still in there to keep her head from hurting," said Myrtle.

But when they walked in the classroom, Bonnie and Amos were the only ones in there.

Bonnie looked worried. "Louvenia was in bad shape last night. You do think she's okay, don't you?"

Amos said, "I told Bonnie that Louvenia was probably running a little bit behind today, that's all. I went ahead and unlocked the classroom for her so that y'all could come in and wait."

Myrtle frowned. "That's very unlike Louvenia to be late and not to have emailed us."

"It's very unlike Louvenia to be wasted at a dinner party," pointed out Miles.

"True. But that was over twelve hours ago."

Amos said, "Maybe she forgot to set an alarm. Considering her condition, and all."

They waited and chatted for thirty more minutes with Myrtle growing more concerned as time went on.

Finally, Myrtle said, "I don't think she's coming. Miles, I think we should check on her."

Miles looked squeamish. "If she's sick, shouldn't we just leave her to recover? We could call her on the phone to check in."

"I want to check in *personally*. After all, I was the hostess last night. I feel a certain responsibility to make sure she's okay," said Myrtle.

Bonnie said, "You don't think it was something she ate? I mean, in addition to the alcohol."

Myrtle said huffily, "We all ate the same thing and the rest of us are fine."

Bonnie blushed.

Miles and Myrtle were back in the car minutes later.

Miles said, "Don't you think you're taking this a little too far? Felix made sure she was tucked in all right last night. This morning is probably a simple combination of a hangover and a forgotten alarm."

"Let's hope so," said Myrtle. "But I'm starting to have my doubts."

Louvenia had a pretty little white house surrounded by meticulous flowerbeds and shrubs. Her car was in the driveway.

"She must have been pretty horrified by your yard yesterday," remarked Miles.

Myrtle said, "Louvenia was probably dying to get her gardening gloves on. Even Dusty is wanting to tackle the yard at this point."

Myrtle gave a firm knock on the front door and then rang the doorbell a few times. They waited. No response.

"Miles, run around to the backdoor and knock there. Maybe that door is closer to her," said Myrtle.

Miles dutifully headed around the back. He returned a couple of minutes later, shaking his head.

"Her car is here. She's not at school. She's not answering the door," said Myrtle. "Let's start looking in through the windows, Miles."

They peered in any uncovered window they could find. Finally, Miles said grimly, "I see her. She's passed out ... I think."

"All right. It's time to call for an ambulance," said Myrtle, pulling out her phone.

Miles said, "I'll call Red, too. The doors are locked and someone will need to break into her house."

Red and the ambulance arrived almost simultaneously. He kicked in Louvenia's front door after his attempts to get her to the door were also unsuccessful. The paramedics took Louvenia away, siren blaring.

He led them over to his police car. "Here. Let's get off the property completely in case there's any foul play. I don't want to mess up a potential crime scene."

Myrtle said, "Naturally, Miles's and my fingerprints will be on windows and doors and doorbells. And Felix took Louvenia home last night, so his prints are sure to be here, too."

Red rubbed his forehead. "Okay, back up. First of all, why are you here to begin with? Isn't it kind of early in the day to be paying visits?"

Myrtle said, "Well, Louvenia didn't show up in class this morning. And she was always the first person there because she liked getting everything set up. She didn't send the class an email to let us know that she was going to be late."

Red raised his eyebrows. "So you just took it upon yourself to be nosy and find out why she wasn't in class? By going to her house instead of phoning or sending her an email?"

Miles coughed. "There was a little more to it than that. Louvenia was at Myrtle's dinner party last night and ... well, she wasn't herself."

"She was drunk as a skunk," said Myrtle.

Red sighed. "I told Elaine not to bring that bottle of wine over."

"That's the funny thing, Red. She must have been drinking before she even came to my house. Puddin proclaimed her intoxicated while I was still cooking dinner. And before dinner, I made sure that Erma was strictly serving coffee."

Red blinked at her. "Erma Sherman was at your party? You invited her? Clearly, I'm going to have to have a full run-down of this dinner party later. Okay, so you think she arrived drunk to your house. Did she drink while she was there?"

Myrtle and Miles looked at each other. "I don't think so," said Myrtle. "But then, I was so busy cooking and serving that I might not have seen her drink."

Miles shook his head. "She didn't have a drop. Not even with dinner. I saw Puddin skip her on purpose and Louvenia didn't even notice."

"What about the food?" asked Red.

Myrtle bristled. "What *about* the food?"

Red sighed. "Don't be sensitive. I mean, did she eat at all?"

Myrtle said, "She was so uncoordinated that she didn't even seem capable. I'm not sure she ate much food at all, if any."

Red pulled out his notebook and jotted down a few notes. "Okay. I'm going to head inside and take a look around and then I'm going right to the hospital. Y'all have done enough for today." He paused and then added grudgingly, "You did the right thing. She looked to be in bad shape. I'll check back in with you later."

Red walked back into Louvenia's house and Miles said, "Now what are we going to do? Our schedule totally opened up without cooking class."

Myrtle thoughtfully considered this. "I think we need to go to Bo's Diner. By now, we'd usually have already eaten some of our classroom creations."

Miles looked perkier. "That sounds like a plan."

"And don't get anything healthy this time! None of that avocado and egg whites stuff. Get some good old sausage and scrambled eggs and hash browns," said Myrtle.

Bo's Diner was packed. As Miles circled the area multiple times, Myrtle remembered why she rarely went to the diner for breakfast. Finally, he was able to park the car and they went inside. It was standing room only in the diner waiting area, but a young man immediately stood and let Myrtle have his seat.

"Age has its benefits," said Myrtle, smiling at Miles as he stood.

Miles looked out the diner window and leaned over. "It looks like Felix Todd is coming in."

"Oh good," said Myrtle. "Let's try to find out what happened last night after he left with Louvenia."

Felix walked in with his usual confident stride. Also as usual, he was impeccably attired with a pink button-down shirt, pink and yellow tie, and light blue pants. He started greeting everyone around him.

Miles said in a hushed voice, "He looks like an Easter egg."

"I think pastels on men is 'in', now," said Myrtle. "Hush. Here he comes."

Myrtle was preparing to reach out and grab Felix's shirt sleeve but to her surprise, he came right over to them.

"Do you know what happened this morning?" he asked them, his features growing suddenly serious.

"To Louvenia, you mean?" asked Myrtle.

"Yes. I was running late this morning, but by the time I got to class, Bonnie told me that Louvenia hadn't shown up and that you two left to try to find her," said Felix.

Myrtle and Miles caught him up. Myrtle asked, "How was Louvenia last night? I mean, how was she on the way home and at her house?"

Felix winced. "We had to stop on the way home and open the car door. Louvenia was ... well, she was sick to her stomach. She also seemed really disoriented and dizzy. I managed to find her keys, get her inside, and laid her on the bed. I left her keys inside, locked the door, and pulled it shut behind me."

Miles nodded. "I could tell she was in bad shape."

"The thing is, that I had absolutely no idea that she drank like that," said Felix. "She was completely out of it. It's a pity, too, because I'd been wanting to ask her about a volunteer project at the church that I'm heading up. I was hoping to get Louvenia involved in it because she's so organized."

Felix looked thoughtfully at Myrtle and she hurried on in case he decided that *she* looked like a good candidate to help with a volunteer project.

"She didn't say anything at all?" she asked.

He shook his head. "Not a word. Except to say that she was going to be sick."

The waitress came up and seated the people ahead of them and then called for Myrtle and Miles.

"Let me know what you find out, will you?" asked Felix.

"I'll be following up with you soon," promised Myrtle.

After breakfast at the diner, Myrtle and Miles felt completely stuffed.

"I can't believe I ate all of that," said Miles as he drove out of the parking lot.

Myrtle said, "A couple of eggs are *good* for you. Gives you protein."

"That wasn't a couple of eggs. That must have been at least a half-dozen," groaned Miles. "And it wasn't just eggs. It was their Super Scrambler. They threw in bacon, sausage, and a lot of different cheeses."

"So you'll just skip lunch," said Myrtle with a shrug.

Miles looked a little ill. "Don't even *mention* lunch."

"Fine. What are we doing now?" asked Myrtle.

"*You* can do whatever you like. I think I need to go home and lie down for a while. I'm not feeling one hundred percent." His eyebrows drew down. "You don't think that I'm in danger from this, do you?"

"What do you mean?" asked Myrtle. "You think Wanda meant you were in danger from high cholesterol? Wanda's not a doctor, Miles. Does she look healthy to you?"

Miles dropped Myrtle off at her driveway and then headed home.

Myrtle worked on a follow-up story for Sloan, worked the crossword puzzle, watched her soap opera with Pasha, and then unloaded the dishwasher from last night. She and Puddin had hand-washed the pots and pans and had used the dishwasher for the plates, but had left the coffee cups and wine glasses and water glasses to be washed the next day. Myrtle stared at them. She had no inclination whatsoever to start loading them all up. Myrtle had half a mind to get Puddin back over there to give her a hand. But it was now suppertime and Myrtle wanted to make herself something to eat. She sighed.

The doorbell rang. Myrtle, glad for a distraction, hurried that way.

"Red!" she said, pushing the door open. "Come on in."

Red came in and plopped down on his mother's sofa. His face was tired.

"What's going on? Something happen?" asked Myrtle.

"Something happened. Louvenia Defore is dead."

"Oh no." Myrtle sat down slowly into her chair. "That seems rather extreme, considering."

"Considering what?" asked Red.

"Considering the fact that she didn't appear to have even drunk any alcohol at all while she was at my house," said Myrtle. "According to Miles, anyway. Puddin wouldn't serve her. She was all judgmental about it."

Red nodded his head. "That fits in with what I saw at Louvenia's house."

"Which was?"

"Louvenia didn't have any bottles of alcohol in her trash. And she didn't have any bottles in her fridge or on her counters. The only alcohol I could dredge up in her house was a dusty bottle of rum located in a far corner of her pantry," said Red. "I don't think she was much of a drinker."

Myrtle frowned. "Not even any red wine to cook with?"

"Oh, there was a bottle of cooking wine in her pantry, but it was unused," said Red.

Myrtle said, "Then I'm confused. Did someone ambush her on the way to my house and force alcohol down her throat?"

"Not exactly. What the state police and I are wondering is whether Louvenia was poisoned while at your house," said Red.

"Poisoned!"

"There are apparently some poisons that create symptoms like drunkenness. Antifreeze was mentioned," said Red, making a face.

Myrtle said, "Someone poured antifreeze in Louvenia's drink at my party? How did they manage that?"

Red shook his head. "I don't really know. I'm here to find out what I can. It does sound weird. Lieutenant Perkins was telling me that manufacturers of antifreeze now have to put a really bitter-tasting component in there so that animals won't accidentally drink it. Remember how it used to be sweet? But now it's more of a bitter taste. I'm not exactly sure how you'd get someone to drink it. And you say that Louvenia didn't even drink any wine?"

Myrtle said slowly, "She didn't. But she did drink coffee. And coffee is bitter."

Red's eyes grew big. "You're right. You served coffee before dinner?"

"Well, Erma did. I was trying to keep the dinner party a little cheaper and not serve a lot of wine. Maybe Erma did it," said Myrtle spitefully.

Red snorted. "You just keep trying to throw Erma under a bus, don't you? She didn't have anything to do with this and you know it. But I do want to talk to her." He made a note in his notebook. Then he rubbed his eyes. "My head is just killing me. This *case* is killing me. There are so many bits and pieces."

"What's one bit or piece?" asked Myrtle, trying not to appear *too* nosy so that Red would answer.

"I've got to chase down some people for accepting bribes from Chester," said Red with a sigh.

Myrtle nodded. She already knew about that, from Louvenia. She tried to act as though this was the first time she'd heard about the bribes. No need to let Red know how well her investigating was going.

Red sighed. "Now we've got Louvenia's death. I just wish we had some kind of evidence here. They say it's going to take a while to analyze Louvenia's blood. Has to be shipped away and whatnot. But I know what a good housekeeper you are."

Myrtle sat very still. She said, "Actually, I'm *not* a very good housekeeper. At least not today. All the pots and pans and plates and silverware are clean and put away ... but I haven't gotten around to the cups and glasses yet."

Red jumped up and walked to the kitchen. He looked at the table and counters full of coffee cups, wine glasses, and water glasses and then turned and beamed at his mother.

"Can you do without coffee cups for a while?" he asked. "And I may have to pack up the other glassware, too, depending on what the forensic guys tell me."

Myrtle shrugged. "Go ahead. I've got a bunch of plastic cups in my pantry that I can use. That's going to be a lot of analyzing, considering I have no idea which cup belonged to Louvenia."

"But it will be worth it. It'll tell us without a doubt what happened to her. Because I don't for a moment think it had anything to do with alcohol," said Red.

He pulled his phone out of his uniform pocket and then paused. "I just remembered—I was going to give you an update on the mower, too. It came in late this afternoon to the shop and naturally I haven't had time to go pick it up. It arrived a lot earlier than that window they'd given me."

Myrtle sighed. "I suppose tomorrow is looking busy too, under the circumstances. How about if Dusty picks it up? He's having to rent one from Tiny now and I bet he'll be delighted to go get it."

Red nodded, "I'll call the store tomorrow and tell them that Dusty can pick it up."

Then he dialed the number for Lieutenant Perkins.

Chapter Seventeen

Myrtle phoned Miles early to fill him in. He came right over and poured himself a cup of coffee. He and Myrtle sat down at her kitchen table.

Miles looked morose. "A crust eaten in peace is better than a banquet partaken in anxiety."

"Would you stop quoting Wanda?" asked Myrtle, glaring at him.

"I thought I was quoting Aesop," said Miles. He gave a big sigh. "I'm sorry about Louvenia. I rather liked her, even though she could be a bit hyper," he said. "But at least your cooking is off the hook."

"My cooking was never *on* the hook. Food doesn't make people appear intoxicated." Myrtle sighed. "What an abrupt and tragic ending to our cooking class."

Miles said, "And I suppose Louvenia isn't our killer, after all. Considering she was murdered, too."

"It would *seem* that way, but remember that we've got to look past what things *seem* and find out the truth. It could be that someone knew that Louvenia had killed Chester and murdered her out of revenge," said Myrtle.

Miles snorted. "And who loved Chester enough to kill someone out of revenge? It seems like he rubbed everyone the wrong way. Hattie was probably closest to him and she's hardly devastated by his death."

"That's true," said Myrtle thoughtfully. "It looks as if we're back to the drawing board. Are you sure you didn't notice anything unusual at my party?"

"I noticed a *lot* that was unusual at your party," said Miles. "That sauce, for one."

"You know what I mean." Myrtle glared at him.

Miles said, "I thought it was unusual for Louvenia to be drunk at a party, also, but we've already gotten to the bottom of that mystery. I thought it was unusual that Hattie was in attendance and that she was relatively pleasant. She always seems sort of hostile and sullen to me."

Myrtle considered this as she bent down to rub Pasha, who had suddenly jumped through the open kitchen window and was now rubbing against her legs. "Maybe Hattie was just happy to get a break from the funeral planning and estate stuff for a while."

"Or maybe she was looking for an opportunity to murder Louvenia," said Miles dryly.

"Good point. Who else was at my party that could be considered a surprise guest?" asked Myrtle. "Felix never misses a chance to hobnob with local voters, so no surprises there."

"Amos," said Miles. "He practically invited himself to your dinner party."

"That's true. He was decidedly hinting at it. And no matter what he says, I can't believe that he was as laid back about losing his health, his wife, his job, and his home as he claims. Maybe he angled for an invitation so that he'd have a chance to kill Louvenia," said Myrtle.

"Yes, but why Louvenia? She had nothing to do with his accident."

"But she might have known something about Chester's death. Maybe she returned to the classroom and saw something

... or realized later that something she'd seen or heard was significant. And we know Louvenia's proclivity for blackmail. She probably figured it was an excellent fundraising opportunity for that new restaurant she wanted," said Myrtle.

Miles sighed. "I was actually starting to look forward to that restaurant. Louvenia could really cook. Okay, so the most unexpected guests were Hattie and Amos."

"Which doesn't really mean anything. We're just guessing. Are you positive you didn't see anything?" demanded Myrtle.

"I didn't see anyone pouring antifreeze in anyone else's drink," said Miles coldly. "And, if you remember, I was fairly busy scraping melted plastic off the stove. Are you sure that *you* didn't see anything? It is your house."

"I was putting out one fire after another," said Myrtle with irritation.

"Yes. Literally," said Miles.

The doorbell rang, startling Pasha who bounded back through the open window.

Myrtle walked briskly to the front door and peered out the front window. She pulled open the door.

"Bonnie!" she said, smiling as she held the door open wide. "Come inside. Miles and I are just having some coffee in the kitchen. Won't you join us?"

Bonnie looked suddenly very anxious, twisting the strap of her purse in her hands. "Oh, I don't know, Miss Myrtle. I think I'm okay. But I'll sit down with y'all for a few minutes if you don't mind."

Bonnie sat awkwardly down in one of Myrtle's kitchen chairs. She looked helplessly at both of them and then burst into tears.

Myrtle was alarmed. "Here, here ... don't do that. Oh, for heaven's sake. Miles, go grab the tissues, will you?"

Miles, eager for an errand, swiftly headed in the direction of Myrtle's bathroom.

Bonnie grabbed the tissues out of his hands as soon as he returned and loudly blew her nose. "I'm so sorry! I just—I heard someone in the grocery store saying that Louvenia had died. I wondered if you knew if it was true and if you knew anything about it. I know she wasn't in class, but I had no idea it was so serious." Her voice broke over the last couple of words.

Myrtle said briskly, "Unfortunately, it's true. Louvenia is dead. What's more, it appears that it wasn't a natural death."

Bonnie's red eyes grew huge. "Not natural? But you don't mean ... she wasn't ... she wasn't *murdered*, was she?"

"I'm afraid so," said Myrtle.

Bonnie said, "First Chester, now Louvenia?" She flushed and said in a low voice, "I can sort of understand about Chester. I don't think he treated people very nicely. But Louvenia was always so nice to everybody. Who would want to kill her?"

Myrtle said delicately, "We don't exactly know. But we do know that it's possible that Louvenia knew something about Chester's death. She was the kind of person who liked to *know* things."

Bonnie's eyes opened wide in alarm. "You think she saw whoever it was that killed Chester?" She shivered. "Miss Myrtle, do you think that Red is going to be talking to … well, everybody in the cooking class again? Does he think it's one of us?"

Myrtle said in a soothing voice, as if talking to a skittish animal, "He's just trying to get information and figure out what's going on, that's all. Did you notice anything odd at my dinner party the other night?"

Bonnie turned red and looked confused.

Miles said, "Aside from the food."

Bonnie, if possible, turned even redder. "Oh! No, everything was fine. Was good! And I don't know that I saw anything *odd*."

"You were saying last time that you wondered if Hattie might have anything to do with Chester's death," said Myrtle.

Bonnie said in a rush, "I shouldn't have said that. I don't know that she was involved at all. And she was nice to me at your dinner. Asked me how I was liking cooking class."

Miles said, "Was there anyone who *was* acting odd?"

Bonnie shifted uncomfortably and Myrtle said in an impatient voice, "You're not testifying in court, Bonnie. You're simply offering an opinion."

Maybe it was the fact that Myrtle had taught Bonnie, but she suddenly stopped hemming and hawing and nodded her head. "Amos was acting weird," she offered.

Myrtle and Miles exchanged a quick glance.

"In what way?" asked Miles with interest.

"I don't know. He talked a lot more. He was … lively. Just different. But he wasn't the only one. Louvenia, of course." Bonnie looked sad. "I *knew* something was wrong. I should have done something—taken her to the doctor. She wasn't acting normal."

"It was probably already too late," said Miles. "I wouldn't feel too guilty over it."

Myrtle said, "Did you see anyone around Louvenia's drink?"

Bonnie knit her brows in concentration. "Actually, I don't think she *had* anything but water."

Myrtle said, "It would have been a coffee cup. Everyone had coffee at the beginning of the evening."

"That's right. No, at least, I didn't notice anything. But everybody was kind of milling around and talking to everybody else. Oh! And eating your tasty hors d'oeuvres."

Miles hid a smile and Myrtle gritted her teeth. *Her* hors d'oeuvres would have been *much* better than Erma's.

"Now what?" asked Miles after Bonnie left. "Amos?"

"Amos, for sure," said Myrtle grimly. "Especially now that Bonnie mentioned he was acting a little off."

"And *we* think he was acting off. Angling for invitations to your dinner party?" Miles looked positively flummoxed at the idea.

Myrtle glared at him. "Trying to get an invitation to one of my dinner parties is *hardly* surprising, Miles. It doesn't mean that the only reason he wanted to be there was because he wanted to murder Louvenia."

"Well, *someone* wanted to murder Louvenia. No one casually attends dinner parties carrying a bottle of antifreeze in his pocket," said Miles.

Myrtle opened her mouth to reply when her phone rang. "I'm so popular today," she muttered. "Hello?"

"Miz Myrtle? Yer lawn look awful."

"Good morning to *you*, too, Dusty. I wish you took such concern over my lawn the rest of the year. Perhaps I should start putting a sign in the grass that says 'mowing courtesy of Dusty.'"

Dusty grunted. "It don't usually look *this* bad."

"Well, I have some good news for you. Red ran by last night and said that the mower is ready at the shop. The only problem is that there's been another murder and he doesn't have time to pick it up."

Puddin would have immediately latched onto the fact that there had been a murder and asked a million questions, offered a million guesses as to the killer, and then would have started incessant gossiping. Dusty, on the other hand, merely grunted again.

"Can I pick 'er up then?" he asked.

"Red said he'd call the shop and authorize you to get it. And I'd appreciate it if you could take care of *my* yard first, since we're funding the mower."

"Whut about ... that stuff. Yonder."

"You mean the yard art? It's all right—it's supposed to be an impermanent display," said Myrtle.

There was silence on the other end as Dusty tried to dissect and digest her sentence. Perhaps, judging from the length of the silence, he was actually diagramming it.

Myrtle said impatiently, "I mean that you can put the gnomes and tools back in the shed."

This time the grunt was more of a groan.

"And I'll be sure to give you something extra for your trouble," said Myrtle with yet another sigh.

She hung up the phone. "The nonsense that I have to deal with from that Dusty and Puddin."

"Keeps you on your toes," said Miles. "So we're seeing Amos now? What's our premise for going to the school when we don't have class?"

"No premise. Just the truth."

"That we're snoopy senior citizens with too much time on our hands?" asked Miles.

Myrtle frowned at him. "No. That I'm an investigative reporter unraveling these mysteries."

"Oh. *That* truth."

In less than an hour, Myrtle and Miles were back at the school, talking to Amos.

Amos tilted his head to one side. "An investigative reporter. Ain't that something?"

"It's a very progressive paper," said Myrtle airily. "They have no problem assigning tough projects to seniors."

Miles snickered and Myrtle punched his toes unobtrusively with her cane. The truth was, of course, that Sloan was deeply committed to assigning Myrtle to the Helpful Hints column, but there was no reason for Amos to know this.

Amos shrugged. "So what is it you want to know? I don't think I really know anything much at all."

Myrtle said, "That's where you're probably wrong. You see, sometimes we know things without really knowing that we know them. Let's start out with what you saw at the dinner party. Did you see anything unusual?"

Amos leaned against his mop, thinking about this for a minute. "Well, I was confused about how Louvenia was so drunk. I didn't even see her drinking any alcohol." He paused. "I didn't really see hardly any alcohol being drunk, *period*."

Myrtle said briskly, "That's because the party was all about the food and not the drinks. You didn't see anyone lingering around Louvenia a lot? Anyone put anything into her drink?"

Amos frowned. "You mean, like, poison her? You're saying she was murdered, then? It wasn't that she had too much to drink?"

Miles shook his head.

Amos gave a low whistle. He absently pushed the mop around the floor for a few moments. "Okay. I did see that young woman talking to her a lot. The cool one."

"Hattie?" asked Myrtle.

"Yeah, that's it. She was talking to Louvenia for a real long time. I thought that was kinda weird. Louvenia and her couldn't have had anything in common, you know?" asked Amos.

Myrtle nodded. "*That's* for sure. It isn't as if they could be comparing tattoo parlors or anything. What could they possibly have to talk about?"

Miles cleared his throat. "There is the fact that Louvenia was Hattie's teacher. They might have been talking about cooking. And there's also the fact that Louvenia was probably the only person at the party that Hattie felt like she really knew."

"Point taken. What else did you see, Amos?"

Amos shrugged and Myrtle said in an encouraging voice. "You know, you're really more observant than you think."

He closed his eyes for a minute as if he was picturing the party in his head. "Felix. I thought at the time that Felix sure was in a hurry to take Louvenia home. Didn't you think so?"

Miles said, "At the time, I was just relieved that Louvenia was leaving before she embarrassed herself—and us in the process."

Myrtle sighed. "And I admit to being concerned that Louvenia might be sick on my carpets. I was glad to see her go, too. But now that I think about it, Felix did seem awfully eager to get Louvenia out of there."

"He was being helpful," said Miles. "I remember thinking that he was risking having the very nice interior of his car messed up by taking Louvenia home. It seemed like a sacrifice."

Miles *would* notice the car.

Myrtle said, "That's the beauty of the plan. Felix did something that *looked* helpful and kind. But maybe he did it to remove Louvenia before we all realized that Louvenia wasn't acting normally and needed help."

Amos said darkly, "If he did that, then he's a very wicked man."

"I can't see it," said Miles. "I've only seen him as someone doing his civic duty in every way."

"Besides, he and Chester were supposed to be such good friends," said Myrtle.

Amos cocked a skeptical eyebrow.

"They played football together in high school and everything," said Myrtle.

Amos gave a decisive shake of his head. "Nope."

Myrtle frowned. "Nope, what?"

"I tried to talk to Felix during a break. Small talk, you know. The man knows nothing about football," said Amos.

Miles said, "Maybe he's just someone who doesn't follow scores or doesn't have a favorite team."

"No, I mean, he doesn't even understand the *game*. Not even the basics," said Amos emphatically.

Myrtle and Miles glanced at each other.

Then Myrtle said, "On a different subject, you've worked with Louvenia for some time, right?"

Amos colored a little. "I wouldn't say worked *with*. I'd say that we worked in the same building. But yes—she's taught these classes every semester for some time now."

"What was your opinion of her, in general?" asked Myrtle.

Amos rubbed the side of his nose. "She was always nice to me. Kind of chatty sometimes, though, when I had work to do."

Miles seemed to think the last sentence was directed at him and he started making 'time to go' motions. Myrtle, on the other hand, held her ground. "Anything else?"

Amos sighed. "Yeah. Hate to speak bad of the dead, or whatever the saying is. But she was kind of sneaky, Louvenia was. I don't think she was completely honest. That might surprise you to hear, since she seemed so professional and all."

Myrtle shook her head. "No, it doesn't surprise me at all. Why do you think she was sneaky?"

"I caught her one time taking an expensive mixer out of the classroom. One of those that probably cost hundreds of dollars. And that was *school* property, not hers," said Amos.

"Did you confront her about it?" asked Myrtle.

"Sure did. Didn't want anyone thinking that *I* took it. Told her to put it back up. She was a real sourpuss about it, too, and real defensive. She was only *borrowing* it, she said. It made me wonder if Louvenia was taking other stuff, too. Or what kind of person she really was," said Amos. "Oh, and one other thing I remembered. Might as well tell you, since you're working on the story or whatnot. The day of that first cooking class, Chester and Felix were arguing. I was cleaning around the corner and they couldn't see me. Chester sounded all cocky like he usually did, but Felix sounded real mad. Something to do with yard signs."

Myrtle said, "Someone else mentioned this. They were talking about campaign signs. I've seen them all over town, supporting Felix's run Was Felix angry that Chester wasn't supporting him?"

Amos shrugged. "I couldn't hear much of it, but that could be true."

Miles frowned. "But Felix was the last one to class that day. You're saying he was arguing with Chester before class even started?"

Amos said, "Yeah. What's more, Chester said something else. Something like 'you better calm down or else I'll tell everybody about you-know-who.' Then Felix stormed past me and left the building. I guess to cool off."

Miles said, "Then he's quite the actor. When he came back in, he was all sunshine and smiles. Even to Chester."

Myrtle nodded. "A politician through and through." She paused. "You know, Amos, this is a lot of stuff to have suddenly remembered."

Amos smiled at her. "I guess I didn't care as much about *who* killed Chester. I was just glad Chester was gone. But now? I dunno. I figured I shouldn't keep stuff to myself. After all, maybe the cops are more suspicious over innocent people since they don't know all the facts."

Myrtle said, "I've got one more question for you, Amos, and then we'll leave you to your mopping. Although I was delighted to have you come to my dinner party, I must admit that I was a little surprised that you wanted to come. After all, you weren't a member of the class. And although you expressed some interest in the class and in cooking, you didn't seem all that interested in the food I served."

Miles gave that odd, muffled coughing sound again and Myrtle glared at him. "Your allergies have *got* to be controlled, Miles. Anyway, as I was saying, I was wondering if you had some sort of ulterior motive for coming to my little dinner."

Amos turned bright red. He looked down at his mop as if it had suddenly become very interesting. "Bonnie," he said, finally.

"Bonnie?" asked Myrtle, very puzzled.

He nodded, glancing up at Myrtle before glancing back down again at the mop. "She reminds me a lot of my ex-wife. In all the *good* ways," he added in a hurry. "I love her smile and that dimple of hers. But here at the school she always ran off during breaks or right after class and I never really got the chance to do more than say hi to her. I thought, if I saw her outside of school, I might have more of a chance to get to know her a little. You see, I saw a horoscope directed to me in the newspaper. Said to seize my chance. Figured it made sense to try to see Bonnie at your party."

Miles said, "And then you ended up at a very unusual dinner party."

"Yes. And I think I probably came across as real pushy or weird or something because I was trying so hard." Amos rubbed his forehead in frustration.

Myrtle crossed her fingers unobtrusively and said, "I'm sure Bonnie didn't think so. And maybe there'll be other opportunities later on for you to meet up with her. It's a small town."

Amos said sadly, "I'd even call and try to ask her out, but I don't have any of her information. Or even her last name."

Myrtle beamed at him. "She happens to be a member of my book club. I've got her number right here in my phone."

"That seems kind of pushy, too," said Amos, looking anxious.

Myrtle said, "Well then, I've got her email address. Just send her a quick email and see what happens."

Amos smiled at her as she handed him a scrap of paper with Bonnie's email and phone number on it. "Thanks, Miss Myrtle."

Chapter Eighteen

Myrtle and Miles walked toward Miles's Volvo. Miles said, "Bonnie said that Amos was acting weird at your dinner party. That's not really a good sign for the future of their relationship."

Myrtle scoffed. "Bonnie wouldn't know flirting if it hit her in the face. But she might understand an email or an invitation to a date a little better. Besides, she's unemployed right now and at loose ends. Who am I to stand in the way of true love?"

Miles gave up. "Okay, well, it's the middle of the day now. Are we going to try and hunt down more suspects? We've got plenty of hours left to do it. What's our next move?"

"I want to find out more about that argument that Felix had with Chester. Let's try to scout him out," said Myrtle, climbing into Miles's car.

Miles said, "How exactly do you propose to do that? We don't just usually run into Felix, do we?"

"We should beard the lion in his den. Let's go right to his house and knock on the door. He knows I write for the paper and we'll just explain that I'm trying to get a little background information for my story," said Myrtle.

Miles started the car, looking worried. "I don't know, Myrtle. He seems like a nice guy, but I doubt your excuse is going to make him want to talk to us. He'll probably come up with some excuse."

"Are you kidding me? He's a politician. All politicians *love* the press."

They drove back to Bradley and right through downtown. Myrtle was looking idly out the window when she suddenly sat up. "Stop the car!"

Miles obediently stopped right in the middle of the street, making a guy in a truck behind him honk at him. He turned red. "I certainly hope there was an emergency that required me to stop in the road."

"You're so *literal*, Miles! I only meant that you should park it. It's Hattie—still speaking to a Realtor, but about to come out. She's another one who's hard to catch up with."

Miles, gritting his teeth, parked the car. Myrtle hopped out and onto the sidewalk in enough time to affect casual surprise when Hattie finally walked out the door of the real estate office.

"Hattie! What a surprise to see you, dear," purred Myrtle. "And you were seeing a Realtor? Are you house shopping?"

Hattie's look of irritation was quickly masked by a tight smile. "It's more like house *selling*."

"I see. Your uncle's home, then."

Hattie said, "Yes. It's a great house, but it's way too big for one person. Not that Uncle Chester would ever admit something like that. And, well, it's just not my style." She gave a shiver as if the white columned, plantation-style home gave her nightmares. Hattie was the sort who probably would prefer to live in a loft in the middle of a big city. "Plus, I heard that the market was very good right now."

Myrtle nodded. Wanda's horoscopes at work again. *Seller's market.*

Then she gave them both a sharp look. "I hope you're not thinking that I'm some greedy relative excited about getting my uncle's money."

Myrtle said, "No, I think you're being smart to talk to a Realtor and start the process of selling."

The defensive look on Hattie's face disappeared. "Sorry," she muttered. "I just heard it from Louvenia and then it made me think that everybody felt the same way."

"When did Louvenia say that?" asked Myrtle, frowning.

Hattie gave a short laugh. "At your dinner party. It was after she'd gotten really smashed, though. She probably wouldn't have said anything otherwise. At the beginning of the party, she was fine and we were talking about local art venues and interesting restaurants. But later, she was telling me that I was low-class and would probably end up spending Chester's money on tattoos. And said something about being cheated out of a restaurant?" Hattie shook her head. "But she was messed up."

Miles said, "Actually, it appears that she wasn't."

"You must not have talked to Red yet. The police chief, that is. But Louvenia is dead," said Myrtle.

Hattie stood very still. "Alcohol poisoning? Overdose?"

"It looks as if she might have ingested antifreeze. She was poisoned," said Myrtle, watching Hattie closely.

Hattie's eyes were hooded now. "Someone murdered her?"

"That's right. Do you have any idea who might have done it? Or why?" asked Myrtle.

"Or did you see anyone hanging around her drink?" added Miles.

Hattie gave a short laugh. "*I* was hanging around her drink. Not really her drink, but her. She was the only person I felt I knew really well enough to talk to. And before she started putting me down, she was sort of entertaining." She shook her head as if she was still trying to figure it out. "Antifreeze. I was wondering how she could be so plastered when I didn't really see her drink anything. I figured she must have had something before she came or that maybe she was on a prescription drug that shouldn't have been mixed with alcohol."

"Did you think anything was strange at all?" asked Myrtle.

"Regarding the people at the party," clarified Miles.

Myrtle glared at him. He was determined to consider her food strange.

Hattie thought for a minute and then shrugged. "Nothing really *strange*. It was strange that she was drunk, but I guess we have an explanation for that. I noticed that Amos seemed to be flirting with Bonnie and I thought *that* was a little odd. I mean, Bonnie's nice and everything, but, you know. And early in the party, Louvenia and Bonnie were talking together for a while. I saw Bonnie start to cry." She shrugged. "I couldn't hear what they were talking about."

"Any ideas why someone would want Louvenia dead?" asked Miles.

Hattie said, "She seemed kind of nosy. Maybe she knew something about Uncle Chester's death." She looked at her watch. "Sorry, but I've got to head out. I've got a lot to do. Good talking to you."

And she was gone.

Myrtle and Miles got back in the car to go see Felix. Felix had a large brick home right on the lake. It had a manicured yard and a couple of nice cars in the driveway. Myrtle and Miles were just getting out of the car when Felix came hurrying outside, carrying a bunch of campaign materials. He paused when he saw them, before putting on a large smile.

"Miss Myrtle and Miles! I keep running into you, don't I?" he asked in a light voice.

Myrtle said, "This time it's not accidental. You probably know that I work for the newspaper," she said.

Felix's eyebrows drew together in thought before he smiled again. "Ah, yes. The Helpful Hints column. Nice stuff. I really like it when you post tips on painting rooms."

"I *meant* my investigative reporting. Sloan relies on me for the really complex stories," said Myrtle with some irritation.

Felix nodded. "Right, right. You write a lot for the *Bugle*, then."

"Yes. And I'm trying to speak to everyone and really flesh out my story. Since Miles and I last spoke to you, we found out a little more about Louvenia's death. She didn't die of natural causes—she was poisoned. Likely by antifreeze," said Myrtle.

Felix dropped a few yard signs and Miles picked them up and handed them back to him.

"Really? I mean ... is that just speculation or something else?" asked Felix.

"Not according to Red. But they're getting the poison pinned down right now," said Myrtle. "What I wanted to ask you was whether you saw anyone hovering around Louvenia's drink or noticed anything at all out of the ordinary."

"Besides Louvenia being intoxicated," added Miles. That always seemed to be the only thing the other dinner party guests noticed.

Felix's face was the very picture of someone earnestly trying to remember. He said slowly, "Bonnie spent a good deal of time with her. And Hattie, of course. And that other woman hovered over her drink."

"Which other woman?" asked Myrtle with a frown.

"The rather pale, sort of squatty one," said Felix. "She was helping you out."

"Oh, Puddin," said Myrtle, waving her hand dismissively. "Yes, she was helping as much as she ever does."

"And Erma, I guess. She was filling everyone's coffee cup," added Felix.

Myrtle nodded. She would *love* to be able to suspect Erma of murder, but she was of the solid belief that Erma, although incredibly annoying and cringe-inducing, was not lethal in any way.

Felix dropped another couple of campaign yard signs and Miles stooped again to pick them up.

Miles was handing them to Felix when Felix said, "Hey, I've got an idea. Why don't you two keep these signs for yourselves? The election is coming up and I can use all the help I can get from my friends in the community."

Myrtle rather thought that 'friends' was a stretch. "I'm afraid I'm apolitical."

Miles hastily nodded. But he wasn't the type to have political advertising marring his immaculate yard.

Felix grinned at them. "That can't possibly be true. I remember your teaching was laced with politics, Miss Myrtle. I think you might even have been a guiding force channeling me into government service."

Myrtle pursed her lips. "I might have been more political decades ago. All I really care about now is rights for seniors."

Miles hid a smile. Myrtle was certainly more political than that. She'd even organized a sit-in at Greener Pastures Retirement Home before.

Felix said eagerly, "Well, that's perfect, then! I'm all *about* rights for seniors."

He then launched into a political spiel as Miles anxiously clutched the yard signs, looking for an opportunity to stuff the unwanted propaganda back into Felix's arms.

Myrtle waited until Felix took a breath and then interjected quickly, "That's wonderful, Felix, and I'm delighted to hear that I inspired your political ambitions. But I'm afraid that my yardman is unhappy enough over my yard art. I dare not put anything else in my yard at this juncture."

Felix looked as though he was about to debate the point, but then stopped. He must have been remembering the 'yard art' and thinking that perhaps he'd rather not have his campaign associated with it, after all.

"I did want to ask you something else. We've heard reports that you and Chester had a disagreement," said Myrtle.

Felix's brow furrowed again. "A disagreement? Whatever over? Chester and I were friends. Everyone knows that."

"Yes, but even friends have disagreements. As a matter of fact, I understood that the disagreements were over the very signs that you're holding right now," said Myrtle.

Felix laughed. "Oh, for heaven's sake. I don't know who was listening or what they heard, but that's completely ridiculous. They misinterpreted everything. Chester wasn't big on having my campaign signs in his yard. That was fine. End of story."

Miles said carefully, "And you weren't upset about that?"

"Maybe I was a little *piqued*. But I certainly understood. So Chester isn't a yard sign kind of guy. That's okay," said Felix, holding out his hands in an expansive gesture.

Myrtle stared at Felix as if he were back in her classroom. "But Chester *was* a yard sign kind of guy. Miles and I have driven past his house plenty of times. There's still a campaign sign in his yard currently that Hattie hasn't pulled up. And the sign is for your opponent."

Felix reddened and said, "It's a free country. Chester could do what he wanted."

"But Chester was your friend. You were counting on him to support you, weren't you?" asked Miles.

Felix gave a short laugh. "I always considered us friends, yes. But Chester was very resentful of my success."

Myrtle said, "But Chester was successful, too."

"But he worked harder for it," said Felix. "He was jealous that I had the opportunity to go off to college when he had to go to work." He paused. "There's really no reason to go into this. Amos is probably behind these crimes. You asked what I noticed at your dinner party. When Chester's name was brought up in passing by Erma, I was watching Amos's face. I don't think I've ever seen such a look of hatred on anyone's face. And this was *after* the man was dead."

Myrtle said, "You didn't bring this up before."

Felix shrugged. "I didn't realize Louvenia was murdered before. Now, if you'll excuse me, I'm going to distribute these signs," he said, taking them back from Miles. If you change your minds about having campaign signs, you know where to find me." He gave them a wink.

"Well, that's all of them," said Myrtle as they got back in Miles's Volvo.

"But not everyone we need to talk to," said Miles.

Myrtle frowned. "Who am I forgetting?"

"Erma. She was there the whole time at your party. She's also fairly observant. And she was the one who was pouring the drinks."

Myrtle said, "That doesn't mean I want to talk to her."

"Don't be so stubborn. You know she's probably got helpful information for us. We don't have to stay long," said Miles.

"Yes, but every second with Erma is like an eternity," said Myrtle darkly.

They drove to Myrtle's and parked in the driveway. Myrtle steeled herself to walk over and talk to Erma.

Miles tried to calm her nerves a little. "Your yard looks nice. Dusty really must have spent most of the day here."

Myrtle stared at her front yard, frowning. "It looks short. Real short. Dusty scalped my lawn. He was so horrified by the length that he took it way too far."

They continued to sit in Miles's car, staring at Erma's house.

"Once we're done, we can go watch *Tomorrow's Promise*," said Miles in the tone of one offering a bribe.

Myrtle said, "All right. Let's do it."

Erma grinned from ear to ear when she answered the door. She fell all over herself letting them into her house. The house currently smelled rather a lot like cooked cabbage and Myrtle's nose wrinkled.

"Myrtle and Miles! Good to see you! Say, Myrtle, your yard looks *so* much better. *Almost* as good as mine, except Dusty cut your grass waaay too short. But so much better!"

Myrtle's head started hurting. And she didn't even have a chance to respond before Erma started up again.

"Are you investigating? What have you found out? Did you need to ask me some questions?" Erma bounced into her living room like a small child at a birthday party, with Myrtle and Miles trailing reluctantly behind her.

Myrtle said, "I'm writing my story for the paper, Erma. One of my investigative pieces—you know."

Erma snorted, an action that seemed to backfire and required her to reach for a nearby tissue box. "Say what you want. I know you're sleuthing. The paper is just a cover." She grinned at them, crumpling up the tissue.

Miles cleared his throat. "What we were particularly interested in, Erma, was the night of Myrtle's dinner party."

Erma nodded excitedly. "Oh, I *know*. Red has already visited me and he was *very interested* in all of my observations. Here, sit down, sit down!"

Erma gave Miles a little shove and he lost his balance, stumbling backward onto a garish loveseat. Myrtle held up her hands as if to say that she needed no such manhandling, and sat sedately in a squeaky armchair.

Erma said, eyes gleaming, "Isn't it just *awful* about poor Louvenia? I mean, we were all *right there* and we had no idea that she was dying the whole time she was at your party, Myrtle."

Miles winced.

Myrtle said briskly, "That's true, Erma, but it's also true that we had no idea that she'd been poisoned. To me, it just looked like she'd had a lot to drink."

"Right, but *where*? Because you weren't really serving it, you know? It was pretty much bone dry at your house. I figured she'd shown up sloshed, but Red said no," said Erma.

Myrtle struggled to regain control over the visit. "Did you see anyone leaning over Louvenia's drink? Or putting anything into it?"

Erma's face was slack with disappointment. "No. I wish I had! If I'd seen someone pouring something weird in Louvenia's drink, I'd have knocked it out of her hand and then yelled to everybody that I'd solved the case and knew who the killer was."

Erma dreamily considered the imaginary happy scenario where Erma Sherman saved the day.

Then she gushed, eyes wide, "And isn't it dreadful that book club killed Louvenia?"

Chapter Nineteen

Myrtle and Miles stared at each other. Even for Erma, this was a non-sequitur.

"What on earth do you mean?" asked Myrtle. "I agree that most of the selections by book club are murder to read. Are you just being facetious?"

Erma gaped at her. "You mean you don't know? But you have to know. You read the book. Miles read the book. You both discussed the book and added your analysis to it."

"What book? What are you talking about?" asked Myrtle, now more visibly irritated. "You don't make any *sense*, Erma."

Erma heaved an exhausted sigh as if Myrtle and Miles's lack of intelligence was very wearing on her. "Bonnie's book club selection. You know! I thought Miles made a great comment that tied right into it. Are y'all both stricken with dementia?"

"Certainly *not*. But I don't know how Louvenia's death is tied into book club in any way," said Myrtle.

Erma brayed the donkey-like laugh that made Myrtle cringe. Then she said, "Clarissa's dog died from antifreeze poisoning."

Myrtle and Miles stared at each other again. It seemed more than coincidental.

Erma mistook their exchanged glance for confusion. "Remember? It was sort of a foreshadowing-thingy, at least according to Tippy."

Myrtle frowned. "Is *that* what Tippy was going on and on about? I couldn't follow her."

"Tippy didn't mention antifreeze by name," said Erma with a shrug. "She just said 'poison.'"

"How *helpful* of Tippy," said Myrtle dryly.

"Perhaps if we'd read the book more closely," said Miles between clinched teeth.

"It must have been a part I skimmed. I do tend to skim during slow sections when the plot lags," said Myrtle with a sniff.

Erma said, "The book club didn't talk much about it, but it was really pivotal to the story. Clarissa was so, so attached to her dog. Millennials are, you know, because most of them don't have kids yet. Although Clarissa was always changing diapers since she had a baby. And then, after Toto died, Clarissa died. That's the whole reason Randolph drank himself to death."

"Right, right," said Myrtle hurriedly, hoping to prevent Erma from giving the book's plot blow by blow. "But I can't imagine anyone in book club killing Louvenia."

"Except Bonnie," murmured Miles under his breath.

"Did the book go into much detail about the effects of antifreeze poisoning? I can't remember," said Myrtle.

"It went on for about a page. They were milking the tragedy of little Toto's death," said Erma helpfully. Then she clapped her hands. "I'm a sidekick!"

Myrtle immediately clarified this. "Honorary sidekick for today. Thank you, Erma. Did you ... um ... happen to share this information with Red?"

Erma shook her head. "No. I was going to, of course. But he was in such a big hurry to get out of here that I didn't have time. You'll pass it on to him, won't you, Myrtle?"

"Of course I will," said Myrtle, a sweet smile on her face.

"You're going to do no such thing," said Miles as they left Erma's house a minute later.

"No. But I didn't need to tell *her* that," said Myrtle as they made the short walk next door. "Come on in. Let's have lemonade and talk and watch our show."

"Homemade lemonade?" asked Miles with a hopeful expression on his face.

"Mix. But you'll never guess it's not homemade," said Myrtle.

Miles sighed.

A few minutes later, they were settled in Myrtle's living room with glasses of lemonade that was a very unnatural yellow, and snacks.

"Let's recap our investigation before we turn on the soap opera," said Myrtle. "We now know that Felix and Chester were arguing over yard signs, no matter how petty that sounds. And we know that Felix thinks Amos was brimming with hatred against Chester because of his workplace injury and how it was handled."

"And we know that someone likely got the idea to kill Louvenia with antifreeze from our illustrious book club selection," added Miles.

Myrtle said, "I don't see Tippy poisoning cooking class teachers somehow. Nor the rest of the book club ... even Georgia. I mean, why *would* they? No, I think either it was Bonnie or it was someone who spoke with Bonnie."

"It just seems sort of random. Why would Bonnie blab about book club to someone not in book club?" asked Miles, shaking his head.

"Because Bonnie is generally an awkward conversationalist. If she can't think of anything to say, she'll say whatever is on her mind. All someone would have to do is engage in conversation with her for long enough to make Bonnie uncomfortable, and she'd be sure to start blabbing about antifreeze, dogs, or whatever else," said Myrtle.

Miles said, "Which means that we need to go back and talk to Bonnie again."

"Exactly. And remember—Hattie said that Louvenia made her cry. Maybe Louvenia was drunkenly trying to blackmail Bonnie and Bonnie desperately needed to get rid of her. Plus, the fact that Bonnie wrote that awful note to Chester; we know how unhappy she was. Her self-confidence was pretty much wiped out by Chester and she told Felix that Chester had messed up her life. Maybe she even lost her teller job because of her lack of confidence. We definitely need to talk to her again. But not until after our soap opera. Even amateur detectives need a break," said Myrtle.

They watched the show together. But by the end of the soap opera, Myrtle was about to make a salient point to Miles about Randolph's new, edgier personality and how that was causing tension with other characters, when she saw Miles had nodded off.

"Miles!" she said sharply. "How could you possibly fall asleep during such an important and exciting episode?"

He rubbed his eyes, but kept them closed. "I haven't slept so well lately. What with being in danger and all."

Myrtle sighed impatiently. "I need to tell Wanda that, in the future, all dire predictions and warnings need to only be directed at me. You don't have the fortitude."

"I think a nap is in order," said Miles, still without opening his eyes.

"It appears that you're already taking one."

Miles slowly opened his eyes and stood, hands dangling loosely. "You're not going to see Bonnie now, are you?"

"I suppose not, since my sidekick is so out of it. How you could fall asleep while Tristan strangled Fernando, I just can't fathom," said Myrtle.

"I'm sure Fernando will return to life in some future episode when they need him for the plot point or to fill some crazy plot hole they've created," muttered Miles. "All right. I'll call you when I've waked up."

"You do that."

When Miles left, Myrtle felt restless. She'd really planned on going back over to talk to Bonnie right away, but now she had to wait. Myrtle loved it when she had leads that Red didn't have yet. Well, it was Red's own fault for not hanging out with Erma for long enough to get a clue.

The doorbell rang and Myrtle frowned at the front door. When she opened it, she saw an exhausted and irritated Miles standing there.

"That must have been the world's record for napping," said Myrtle. Then she noticed that Miles carried a small overnight bag.

"My air conditioner is broken. It must have been broken since this morning to be as hot in there as it is," said Miles. He walked into Myrtle's living room and sat heavily on the sofa.

"Did you call the repair place?" asked Myrtle.

"They're already closed." The sentence came out as more of a moan.

"Well, then, you can call them first thing tomorrow and see if Jim can fit you in." She looked at the bag. "And you're moving in, in the meantime?"

"Since you have air conditioning and an extra room, I suppose so," said Miles ungraciously. "Although it's going to make Erma Sherman gossip about us again."

"But no one wants to spend enough time in Erma's company to *hear* the gossip, so it will be fine," said Myrtle.

"I can't believe there's no afterhours answering service for the repair shop," grumbled Miles.

"For heaven's sake, Miles! This isn't Atlanta. You've got a place to stay, so calm down. I don't usually have to talk you off the cliff like this. You're cranky and need to take a nap—please retreat to the guest room and take one!"

Miles obediently stomped off down the short hall leading to the guest room. Five minutes later, Myrtle remembered that there wasn't a blanket in there. Miles was already sound asleep when she tossed the blanket over him.

Myrtle looked impatiently at her watch an hour later. It was already getting dark and she wanted to call on Bonnie at a reasonable time of day. It would certainly be a lot easier, too, if Miles drove her there. It was a bit of a way to walk.

She walked into the guest room. "Miles?" she asked.

No response.

"Miles!"

This time he grunted in his sleep, but still didn't wake up.

That settled it. If her sidekick was too sleepy, she was going to have to be the one to interview Bonnie, by herself. Otherwise, Erma would decide to show off her book club knowledge and call Red on the phone to tell him all about the antifreeze.

As she was getting her keys, she heard a cat yowling outside. Pasha was telling her she was hungry. And, if she didn't immediately feed her, Pasha would continue her discordant concert outside the house.

Myrtle opened the kitchen window so that Pasha could come and go as she pleased. "What does my sweet baby want for her dinner, hmm? Maybe a tuna can? Or a chicken can? Or beef?"

Pasha purred at her as if to say that all of the above would suit her fine.

Myrtle prepared a heaping plate and left Pasha happily eating. She hurried out the door as the sun started setting.

It wasn't really that Bonnie's house was that far away. It was just that everyone seemed surprised to see Myrtle walking down the street toward town. They must have gotten used to seeing Myrtle being chauffeured by Miles. Three different cars stopped and asked her if she needed a ride. One of them was an old biddy even more elderly than Myrtle. Myrtle decided that she'd rather walk for miles instead of accepting a ride from Petunia. But it was good to know that she could easily find someone to drive her in case Miles couldn't.

When Myrtle finally arrived at Bonnie's door, she rapped and rang the doorbell. Bonnie's startled face peered out a minute later.

"Why, Miss Myrtle? Whatever are you doing here?" Bonnie opened the door wide and looked outside. "Did you *walk* here?"

Myrtle frowned. "Why does everyone persist in thinking that I'm incapacitated? I'm perfectly capable of walking wherever I want to walk."

Bonnie's eyes lingered on Myrtle's cane and Myrtle said, "This thing? This cane simply helps me with my balance. But I'm glad you're here, Bonnie. There are some questions I need to ask you."

Bonnie was practically wringing her hands. "What is it? Is something wrong?"

"There's just a couple of different things I wanted to ask. For one, you were seen crying during a conversation with Louvenia. Could you tell me what that was about?" asked Myrtle.

Bonnie knit her brows, trying to remember. "Oh, wait. It must have been during your party. Before Louvenia got too drunk. She was drunk enough to start talking about things, though. She was telling me that she lost her little dog, Pepper, right before cooking class started. I *loved* Pepper. Louvenia used to have him in the car with her when she ran errands and she'd go through the bank drive-through with him. I'd give him dog biscuits through the window. So sad." Her eyes clouded even now, thinking about it. Then she said, "But you didn't really come here to ask about Pepper, did you?"

Bonnie was simply too tenderhearted. Myrtle sighed. "I thought Louvenia might have been upsetting you in another way. On to my next question. You see, Bonnie, I did read your book club book. I really did. I simply read it very *quickly* and if there was a section that I thought was dragging, I might have skimmed a little. I completely missed the importance of the fact that Louvenia was poisoned with antifreeze."

Bonnie flushed, leaving blotchy red spots on her cheeks. "I see. And you think because I read the book and I was in the cooking class and at your dinner party, that I must have murdered Louvenia."

Myrtle was very worried that the tears that were filling Bonnie's eyes were about to spill over. "No, no. Not necessarily, Bonnie."

Bonnie flung her hands out beseechingly. "Because how stupid would I be to do something like that? Do people really think I'm that dumb? Red hasn't found out yet, but he will. I'm sure the way that Louvenia died is going to get out soon and then everyone in book club is going to think that I killed Louvenia. And probably Chester, too!"

Myrtle said soothingly, "That's exactly why we need to find out who the responsible person is. Now I need you to think carefully, Bonnie. Really focus. I know you enjoyed the book you picked for club and you probably talked to people about it. With whom did you speak?"

Bonnie gave a tremulous sigh. "Oh, goodness. Sometimes I just babble, you know?"

"Think!" commanded Myrtle in her best former-school-teacher tone.

Bonnie wrinkled up her forehead as if thinking were a painful process. She slowly said, "Tippy and I talked a lot about it. Or, I guess, I was the one telling Tippy about it."

Myrtle felt a headache coming on. They were going to be there all night if Bonnie listed the completely innocuous people in book club. "Tippy Chalmers isn't likely to be on top of our suspect list. Did you mention the book to anyone in class one morning, maybe? Maybe one day when you were there early and trying to make conversation?"

Bonnie buried her face in her hands as if trying to force the information from her head. "I ... I did mention it to Amos. He was trying to talk to me on the way into class one morning and I didn't know what to talk about." She lifted her head and looked helplessly at Myrtle. "Amos just sent me an email, too, a little while ago. I don't know how he even had my address!"

Myrtle sighed. "Bonnie, Amos likes you."

The remainder of Bonnie's face turned scarlet. "No. No, he couldn't."

"He could and he does. Now, I don't like getting messed up into your private business, but it seems as though you need everything laid out for you since you're not one to pick up on subtleties. Amos likes you. He would like to go out with you. Your own horoscope implored you to open your eyes," said Myrtle.

Bonnie's eyes were now wide open behind her thick glasses.

Myrtle said, "Now you know. If you don't feel the same about Amos, you can easily tell him that you're just not interested."

"But I *am*! I just didn't realize—didn't know." A glow seemed to settle around Bonnie.

Myrtle hastily interrupted the glowing. "That's great, Bonnie. You should answer the email then. Now, let's get back to these questions. You thought Amos was acting oddly, but now you realize that he was just awkwardly trying to make conversation with you because he would like to pursue a relationship. Was there anyone else that you mentioned the book to?"

"Hattie was walking by when I was talking to Felix about the book club book and the antifreeze," said Bonnie slowly. "She might have overheard what I was saying. But I didn't *tell* her. I didn't think she seemed very much like a book person."

"I don't know—she sort of looks like the kind of person who might go to poetry readings and such. You're doing a good job. Is there anyone *else*?" asked Myrtle.

Bonnie frowned in concentration again and then smiled. "Felix! But I didn't have to tell him about the book. He was already reading it. He came in right after Hattie when I was still talking to Amos. Felix said that he'd been reading the same book and was really enjoying it, even if the title had escaped him. I gave him the title and then we talked about the book for a while."

So, basically, Bonnie had informed everyone in the class one way or another about the antifreeze poisoning. Myrtle's head hurt even more.

Chapter Twenty

It was fairly dark when Myrtle left Bonnie's house, and there wasn't as much traffic on the road. It wasn't far into her trip home when a car pulled up alongside her.

Tippy Chalmers rolled down her passenger window. "Myrtle! What on earth are you doing walking around at this hour?"

"I frequently walk around at night," said Myrtle with some irritation, "it's just that I'm usually closer to home than this."

"Well, hop in. I'll drive you back to your house. For goodness sake."

Myrtle climbed into the leathery luxury of Tippy's Cadillac.

Tippy said, "Couldn't someone have driven you over and back? Elaine or maybe Miles?"

"I don't really mind walking," protested Myrtle. She was about to go on a rant about how people underestimate seniors when she suddenly decided to spend her time more productively. "Tippy, you know everything that goes on at the church, don't you?"

"Goodness. I don't know about *everything*," said Tippy.

"Except that you've basically been an unpaid, unglorified volunteer over there for the past twenty years and in every aspect of the church's running," said Myrtle.

"Well, I wouldn't have put it *that* way, Myrtle, but yes, I do seem to have a hand in nearly everything that goes on over there." Tippy suddenly turned to look at Myrtle with wide, delighted eyes. "Are you interested in volunteering? Because I can put you on the Chancel Guild."

Myrtle hastily said, "Unfortunately, I don't have time for volunteering right *now* and usually when I do, it's Red who signs me up, as you know. That's just tradition. No, what I wanted to ask you was about Felix."

Tippy raised her eyebrows. "Is *Felix* interested in volunteering at the church?"

Myrtle said, "Would that be an extraordinary event?"

"It certainly would. Oh, he talks about helping there, and I'm sure he'd like to have the chance to do a little politicking at the church. But so far, it hasn't come to fruition."

Myrtle said, "So what if Felix were to say that he was contacting someone about helping with a project he was overseeing at the church?"

"Then I'd say he'd suffered a small stroke," answered Tippy, succinctly.

Myrtle thought about the fact that Felix wasn't a football player and was actually rather clumsy. And the way he'd fibbed about the church. How he'd forgotten the title of the book he was reading. And the way he so solicitously took Louvenia home from Myrtle's dinner party before anyone noticed anything amiss. Myrtle's lips tightened into a thin line.

Myrtle's cell phone started ringing, making her jump.

It was Elaine. "Myrtle, I hate to ask you, but do you mind coming over and keeping an ear out for Jack for an hour or so? He's asleep, so it shouldn't be any trouble. Red has been insistent about not going to the doctor for the last couple of days, but now he has this raging fever. I need to drive him to the urgent care before they close."

"Of course! I'll be right there," said Myrtle. She said to Tippy, "If you could drop me by Red's instead. I need to help with Jack for a little while."

Tippy said with a smile as she pulled on Myrtle's street, "They're lucky to have you."

"And vice versa. Well, except for the fact that Red gets on my nerves sometimes."

Tippy dropped Myrtle off at Red's house as Elaine was walking out the door with a very grouchy, flushed Red.

The house was quiet with Jack sleeping soundly in the back. Myrtle thought about napping herself, but her mind was racing too much with information. She watched a couple of evening game shows, winning them all easily.

It took longer than they'd expected to get Red home. There was a long line of people still ahead of them at the urgent care, even though Red was the last patient they accepted. By the time he was seen and they'd traveled to the next town to the 24-hour pharmacy, it was eleven o'clock.

"Sinus infection," said Elaine, a knowing smile on her face.

"Which probably got worse through all the aggravation at the urgent care," growled Red.

"Everything all right here?" asked Elaine.

"Just fine. Jack is sound asleep and I won a pot of money on the game shows."

"Too bad it's not real," said Red. "Especially after all the medical bills we racked up tonight. Need me to walk you back home?"

"Across the street? Certainly not. I'll be just fine. You take your medicine and turn in," said Myrtle. "Besides, I've got a houseguest over there. Miles doesn't have air conditioning."

Elaine said, "Oh good. I was going to ask you about that. I thought I saw someone outside your house when we drove by."

"He was passed out asleep when I left." Myrtle frowned.

She paused for a moment, wondering whether she should share what she'd found out from Tippy and Bonnie and what she now thought about Felix. But the tiredness in Red's eyes as well as his obvious fever made her decide to keep it to herself until tomorrow. Then she could reveal how she'd solved everything.

Myrtle walked across the street and up the walkway to her front door. She sighed as she passed by the scalped yard and fished her keys out.

She quietly let herself in, in case Miles had gone back to sleep. She was feeling tired herself and wasn't exactly in the mood to rehash her visit with Bonnie or to hear any recriminations for ditching her sidekick to go.

Myrtle frowned as she walked into the living room. The house was completely dark. But Elaine said she'd seen someone outside her house. Surely Miles would have had the good sense to turn on a few lights for her before she came back home.

She walked toward the desk and the light on top of it, being careful to lean on her cane as her eyes adjusted to the darkness. Before she clicked it on, she heard a low growl and her heart jumped into her throat.

It was Pasha. But Pasha's fur was standing on end and her teeth were bared as she continued growling and staring toward the hall to the bedrooms.

Pasha wouldn't growl at Miles. She liked Miles a whole lot more than Miles liked her, actually.

Myrtle walked as quietly as she could down the short hall, carefully avoiding the squeaky floorboard as Pasha stayed in the living room.

She heard a squeaking sound, like bedsprings. Myrtle rushed into the guest room, flipping on the overhead light.

And saw Felix Todd holding a pillow to Miles's face.

Chapter Twenty-One

Felix turned to look at her, astonished.

Myrtle turned the light back off and swung her cane at Felix, hard. She connected to him somewhere and he let out a stream of profanity and lurched toward her. Myrtle swung again at him, making contact but not nearly as hard. She stumbled away to run toward the living room and front door.

Her knowledge of her home's layout was a plus and she carefully skirted any objects in her way, hurrying toward the door. The profanity behind her grew louder as Felix ran into Myrtle's armchair. Then he started screaming and Myrtle glanced behind her to see that Pasha had leaped from Myrtle's desk onto Felix's back and was screeching about as loudly as Felix was.

To her great relief, Miles appeared from the hallway, glasses askew and eyes wide.

"Call Red!" said Myrtle as Felix tore Pasha off of his back, stumbling almost drunkenly in the process and crashing into Elaine's hideous gnome. He hit the floor with a resounding thud, knocking his head against Myrtle's coffee table as he went down.

"People is clumsy," said Myrtle thoughtfully, remembering what Wanda said. And then, "No hurry, Miles. He's seeing stars. And I want to talk to him for a few minutes before Red comes over."

Felix groaned from the floor.

"Don't try anything, Felix. Miles and I make a formidable team. I *would* give you a glass of water, but since you're an uninvited guest, I think we'll just skip the formalities. Plus the fact that you tried to kill Miles, of course."

Miles, considering he was so close to death, seemed only mildly miffed.

"I wasn't trying to kill Miles," said Felix coldly.

Myrtle said, "Oh, I know. You were trying to kill *me*. Quite unsuccessfully, I might add. And you must have gotten a lot of bumps and bruises from climbing in the kitchen window. That was only meant to be a portal for Pasha."

Felix didn't answer.

"The nice thing is, that you so solidly incriminated yourself. Attempted murder of Miles with me as witness? What a mess. You see, all I really had was circumstantial evidence," said Myrtle.

Felix remained sulkily silent.

Miles said, "I'd like to hear the circumstantial evidence. A lot must have happened while I was asleep."

"Not much, actually. Short conversations with Bonnie and Tippy. What *did* happen is that I had a series of epiphanies," said Myrtle.

"Which were?" asked Miles.

Felix's normally friendly face scowled at Myrtle.

"That Felix wasn't good at telling the truth. He lied about playing football with Chester in high school, for one."

Felix's eyes glinted. "That was a slight exaggeration. Hardly a criminal offense."

"You're not really the most *coordinated* person, so I should have guessed earlier that you weren't telling the truth. You also lied about Louvenia. You said that you wanted to speak to her about a volunteer project at the church. But Tippy Chalmers, who knows *everything* about what goes on at the church, said you weren't very involved over there. Another example of your not telling the truth," said Myrtle.

"White lies," shrugged Felix, sitting up cautiously. "The kind of thing most politicians do. I merely was avoiding a lengthy explanation."

"Of course, there was the fact that you hustled Louvenia out of my dinner party very quickly to make sure no one got help for her," added Myrtle.

Felix didn't even try to argue this point. His face was drawn and exhausted and he gave another shrug.

Myrtle adopted her former schoolteacher voice again and Felix straightened up a bit on the floor. "You mentioned that Chester was resentful of your success, but wasn't it the other way around? You took the time and effort to get a college degree and, if I remember correctly, even graduate work. But he made a fortune without those things. Did that make you feel as if you'd put in the time and effort and deserved to do better than Chester?"

Felix said in a tired voice, "Of course it did. I put in an investment in education and deserved the outcome I had."

Miles said, "But he put in an investment, too. His investment was just physically hard work instead of education."

"So you already felt resentful of him, and then it was really the icing on the cake when he didn't even support his old school friend in the local election. You *expected* his support. After all, if one of your *friends* didn't support you, what did that say about your qualifications? You probably started off being low-key about it, didn't you? But then Chester escalated it by laughing at you. Plus, Chester pushed back. We heard that he threatened you with blackmail," said Myrtle.

Felix's lips tightened. "He happened to see me with someone. He simply misinterpreted what he'd seen."

Miles said, "But a misinterpretation could really cost you, couldn't it? All the campaign signs and literature that I've seen portray you as a big family man."

"You were desperate to keep Chester quiet about your affair. Especially this late in the campaign. So instead, you took the opportunity to kill him after class." Myrtle paused, looking thoughtfully at Felix. Dressed in carefully-pressed dark slacks and a pastel button-down showing under a dark jacket, it was hard to picture him with a pillow over Miles's face. She went on in a harsher voice, "He was probably expecting an argument, not being murdered by you. You don't look like a killer. The element of surprise would have worked in your favor, since Chester was a much larger man than you are."

"Size wasn't a factor in Louvenia's death, though," noted Miles.

"No, it wasn't. And poisoning ... I'm surprised you went in that direction. I'd have thought you'd have been much more likely to do what you just tried with Miles. Smothering doesn't really leave much of a trace, does it? It would look as though he'd just passed away in his sleep."

Miles gave a small shiver.

"But after a friendly conversation with Bonnie before class one day, you realized that antifreeze could be an effective poison. What's more, it's easily accessible to everyone. I bet if Red widens the search to out of town stores, he'll discover that you made a purchase of antifreeze in anticipation of my dinner party. Probably purchased in one of those big box stores far away where no one would have known who you were," said Myrtle. She shook her head. You should have followed the advice in your horoscope: *avoid leaving town.*

Miles said, "And you chose the dinner party when all the other suspects would be there."

"A stroke of genius on my part," said Felix in that same, tired voice.

Myrtle couldn't tell if he was being sarcastic or not. She continued, "How did Louvenia know it was you who killed Chester? Did you think that she'd gone for the day and then, when she returned, she caught you trying to wipe down the meat thermometer for prints?"

Felix gave a short laugh. "I don't know. That's what must have happened, I suppose. She never told me how she knew. But she wasn't bluffing—she definitely knew."

"And then she tried blackmailing you with the information. The same method that got Chester killed. You must have felt that you had only one choice," said Miles thoughtfully.

Myrtle said, "You were probably trying to figure out how to get rid of Louvenia when two things happened almost simultaneously. You received an invitation from me for a class dinner party and Bonnie Pendergrass told you about the antifreeze poisoning incident in her book club selection."

"And that took care of Louvenia's blabbing," said Miles. "What I'm still not clear on is why you tried to murder Myrtle a few minutes ago."

Pasha growled at Felix from the doorway, her eyes gleaming with fury.

Felix sighed. "A moment of madness? I had dinner downtown and decided to leave my car down there and take a walk to clear my head. I passed your house and all the lights were off. None of the neighbors were out and about and it was totally quiet on the street. I walked around the back of the house and saw you had a window open."

"But *why*?" asked Miles.

"Because, Miss Myrtle was the toughest teacher I ever had, and that counts grad school. She was determined, stubborn, dogged. There was a paper that I didn't hand in once." He laughed. "Miss Myrtle had a zero-tolerance policy on late work. The paper was already late and I knew I was going to get a zero on it, so why turn it in? But she *made* me turn it in. Said it was important that I knew how to write a paper and not stall on writing one simply because I wasn't sure how to start. She kept on me and kept *on* me and I turned it in," said Felix.

"And she gave you a good grade?" asked Miles, always one to look for the happy ending.

"No, I gave him a zero," said Myrtle sharply. "It was my policy. But that didn't mean he didn't have to do the same amount of work as everyone else in the class."

Miles said, "I'm confused. The research paper made you decide to smother Myrtle in her sleep?"

"The research paper incident made me realize that Miss Myrtle was like a dog with a bone. She doesn't give up. She's the perfect investigative reporter for the newspaper because she's completely bullheaded. Plus, I thought she was starting to see the truth. The last thing I needed was for her to uncover two murders," said Felix.

"My son is pretty bullheaded, too. I think you'd have found that Red would have been on your trail, even if you *had* succeeded. But let's find out how close he was to figuring it out," said Myrtle.

And Miles made the phone call.

Red was over there immediately in a hastily-pulled-on and wrinkled uniform. He secured Felix and called Lieutenant Perkins.

"Really, Felix? You were trying to kill my mother?" he asked in disgust after he got off the phone with the state police.

Miles said, "And doing a remarkably poor job of it, if it's any consolation."

Myrtle said, "We left the crime scene as-is, so you could see how everything transpired."

Red's gaze went from the bruises and cuts on Felix to the hideous gnome with the now-broken hands to the askew armchair. "It looks like a bar fight happened in here."

"Just wait until you see the mess in the guest room. And be sure to tell Elaine that her gnome was a huge help in catching the perpetrator," said Myrtle. "Pity it got injured."

Red studied the gnome again and winced. "Yes, isn't it?"

He hauled Felix to his feet and walked him out the door, past a still-growling Pasha.

"Mama, I'll come back for a chat after I've booked Felix," Red said. "You won't be asleep, will you?"

"Hardly." She had an important story to write for Sloan. "Shouldn't *you* be asleep?" She glanced at Miles. "Red is sick with a fever."

Miles turned pale and slowly backed away from Red. A moment later, he was patting his pockets for his bottle of hand sanitizer.

"I'll be better soon," said Red. "I think that antibiotic is already kicking in."

Red left with a limping Felix.

Miles looked after them thoughtfully, rubbing the sanitizer over his hands. "You seem to have quite disabled Felix. That's pretty impressive. He's a good thirty years younger than you are."

"Adrenaline," said Myrtle with a shrug. "And sheer vexation. He was trying to kill my sidekick. What total impudence! He couldn't be allowed to get away with it."

"Although *you* were the intended victim," reminded Miles again.

"How anyone could confuse the two of us is baffling," said Myrtle with a snort.

"It was very dark. And there was no moon outside. A lump under the covers was probably just like any other lump under the covers," said Miles.

"I must say it was about time. I was *always* the one in danger. A sidekick *should* pick up the slack," said Myrtle.

"I suppose. I'll happily let you take on the danger again next time, though. What's next?"

Myrtle said, "I write the big scoop for the paper and call Sloan to make him fit it in as the top headline. You go to sleep and call the air conditioning guy in the morning."

"That's it?" asked Miles.

"Don't tell me this case has made you an adrenalin junkie, Miles."

Miles said, "Even though I didn't want to sign up for the cooking class, I have to admit it did turn out to be very exciting."

"I told you it would," said Myrtle smugly.

"Maybe we can look at the rest of the course catalog," said Miles. "But next time we'll sign up for something less thrilling. And far less dangerous. Like skydiving."

About the Author:

Elizabeth writes the Southern Quilting mysteries and Memphis Barbeque mysteries for Penguin Random House and the Myrtle Clover series for Midnight Ink and independently. She blogs at ElizabethSpannCraig.com/blog, named by Writer's Digest as one of the 101 Best Websites for Writers. Elizabeth makes her home in Matthews, North Carolina, with her husband. She's the mother of two.

Sign up for Elizabeth's free newsletter to stay updated on releases:

https://elizabethspanncraig.com/newsletter/

This and That

I love hearing from my readers. You can find me on Facebook as Elizabeth Spann Craig Author, on Twitter as elizabethscraig, on my website at elizabethspanncraig.com, and by email at elizabethspanncraig@gmail.com.

Thanks so much for reading my book...I appreciate it. If you enjoyed the story, would you please leave a short review on the site where you purchased it? Just a few words would be great. Not only do I feel encouraged reading them, but they also help other readers discover my books. Thank you!

Did you know my books are available in print and ebook formats? And most of the Myrtle Clover series is available in audio. Find them on Audible or iTunes.

Please follow me on BookBub for book recommendations and release notifications: https://www.bookbub.com/profile/elizabeth-spann-craig .

I have Myrtle Clover tote bags, charms, magnets, and other goodies at my Café Press shop: https://www.cafepress.com/cozymystery

If you'd like an autographed book for yourself or a friend, please visit my Etsy page.

I'd also like to thank some folks who helped me put this book together. Thanks to my cover designer, Karri Klawiter, for her awesome covers. Thanks to my editor, Judy Beatty, for all of her help. Thanks to beta readers Amanda Arrieta and Dan Harris for all of their helpful suggestions and careful reading. Thanks, as always, to my family and readers.

Other Works by the Author:

Myrtle Clover Series in Order (be sure to look for the Myrtle series in audio, ebook, and print):

Pretty is as Pretty Dies
Progressive Dinner Deadly
A Dyeing Shame
A Body in the Backyard
Death at a Drop-In
A Body at Book Club
Death Pays a Visit
A Body at Bunco
Murder on Opening Night
Cruising for Murder
Cooking is Murder
A Body in the Trunk
Cleaning is Murder
Edit to Death
Hushed Up
A Body in the Attic (2020)
Southern Quilting Mysteries in Order:
Quilt or Innocence

Knot What it Seams

Quilt Trip

Shear Trouble

Tying the Knot

Patch of Trouble

Fall to Pieces

Rest in Pieces

On Pins and Needles

Fit to be Tied

Embroidering the Truth (2020)

The Village Library Mysteries in Order:

Checked Out

Overdue

Borrowed Time (2020)

Memphis Barbeque Mysteries in Order (Written as Riley Adams):

Delicious and Suspicious

Finger Lickin' Dead

Hickory Smoked Homicide

Rubbed Out

And a standalone "cozy zombie" novel: Race to Refuge, written as Liz Craig

Made in the USA
Columbia, SC
26 September 2023